Coming Out of His Shadow

Carmen Yvette Jones

Coming Out of His Shadow
Copyright © 2018
Carmen Yvette Jones First Edition
ISBN: 1546917403
ISBN-13:9781546917403

Graphic designer front and back cover by: Maurice Jones
Editing by: Melane Bower

Printed by CreateSpace

This is a work of fiction. Names, characters, businesses, places,
events and incidents are either the products of the author's
imagination or used in a fictitious manner.
Any resemblance to actual persons, living or dead, or actual
events is purely coincidental.

DEDICATION

I dedicate this book to my parents, Edward M. Jones and Dorothy Jones. Both are gone too soon, yet they still live within me and I believe they are still helping to guide me through my journey of life. I am grateful to have experienced life with two Godly parents.

I will carry with me so many fine memories of them both..

CONTENTS

ACKNOWLEDGMENTS

I give praises to God, who is first in my life, for without him I can do nothing. It is in his timing that he unlocked what he had hidden inside of me, and now it's time to give birth.

I give my love and a special thank you to my two sons, Joseph and Frank Jr., for all the confidence you had in me.

To my sisters, Elaine A. Simpson, Joanne Alston, and Dorothy R. Williams, thank you for being my sisters. I appreciate you and all the encouragement you have given me throughout my life.

To my nieces, Leila Sawyer, Ashley Harris and Simone Williams, thank you for your support.

To my friends, Rosalind Nelson, Penny Holloman, Jontau Weeks-Carter, Jeff Giddings and Anthony Hosendorf, thank you for listening ear and your encouragement to continue to write.

ONE

Sheila wakes up to what she thought would be just another day.

She gets out of bed, gets on her knees to pray, then makes the bed before taking a shower and walking into her closet to select clothes for work.

Before leaving the house that morning, she pulls out a package of chicken from the kitchen freezer to defrost for that night's dinner. She picks up her keys from the hallway table, glances at herself in the mirror, and sets the house alarm. Once outside, she gets in her car to head to her new job of four months.

Sheila is an administrative assistant at an investigation agency, her job consisting of creating and maintaining the investigators' schedules as well as compiling and organizing their clients' case files. She had once worked as a paralegal for Bailey & Bailey, a large, prestigious law firm. It had been a good, solid firm, one that had been in practice for over 25 years.

Sheila worked on various cases, everything from divorce to criminal cases, and had learned a lot during her five-year career there. Her responsibilities as a paralegal consisted of gathering case facts by investigating leads and theories.

But the changing economy had forced Bailey & Bailey to downsize, and Sheila had been one of 100 people who were laid off, taking the firm from 300 employees down to 200. Sheila received a generous severance package, so for a while she sat back and enjoyed not having to get up early in the mornings.

Sheila Moore, 34, and John Moore, 35, have been married for ten years. They've had a good, normal life, and though they don't have the house with a white picket fence, many others might think they want what Sheila has.

They live in a single-family, beige brick house, with a two-car garage and a nice front porch. They were lucky in finding this house in a good neighborhood. However, this house is far from being a home.

Now, if you didn't know Sheila was married, you would have thought she was single. In the beginning of their marriage, John had told her that everything needs to remain separate, especially their finances. John is a no-nonsense kind of man who says what he means and means what he says. He always had a thing about money, which was why he preferred that they keep it all separate.

Sheila could not understand why, but she agreed.

They rarely go out together, because John is always working. His job as a supervisor with a local, well-known construction company pays well, in addition to his own business as a handy man. He always says the business is what keeps his skills up, besides being a way to earn some extra money.

But his constant working is the reason their marriage has run into some problems. Sheila has been feeling neglected and lonely, not to mention that she also feels her clock ticking and has told John that she wants to have a baby.

John, however, has told her that he is not ready to begin a family and that they can't afford to have a child now. In their last conversation about it, Sheila argued that there will never be the "right time," reminded him that they're not getting any younger, and that she wants to start a family next year.

Sheila had been home, unemployed, for three months and was beginning to feel lonely and bored. There had been times where she caught herself imagining what it would be like to have a baby in the house. She felt that, at least if there was one, she wouldn't be quite so lonely. You see, Sheila grew up dreaming of her wedding day and having children as well as a career, but John is denying her, her one last dream to have his child.

And besides that, all her friends were working, and she had no one to talk to or go out to eat with. So after applying for and receiving unemployment compensation while watching what was left of her severance money, she started looking for a new job. She soon discovered, that finding a new job was not always so easy, and before she knew it three months had turned into five months.

She applied to other law firms, but they too were downsizing and not looking to hire. She had been forced to branch out into other types of work, which was how she finally landed the job at Smith & Gilford Private Investigators, whose clients range from superstars to the average person and with cases ranging from cheating spouses to company scandals.

So far, Sheila has learned a lot about investigating, as well as the equipment investigators use. One day, Mr. Gilford approached her at the front desk and asked her if she would be interested in doing some investigating on her own, and she excitedly said yes.

Sheila was always a fast learner, especially when it came to something she enjoyed doing. Sheila's happy working at Smith & Gilford Investigators Agency as an administrative assistant, which is how she learned the ins and outs of being an investigator—everything from how to use a long lens camera to using a pen as a listen device. But nothing made her happier than hearing Mr. Gilford offer her a once in a life time chance to become an investigator, a dream she'd never thought of. And she can't wait to see John and tell him her good news.

Coming home from work at the end of the day, Sheila goes into the kitchen to start her dinner. The chicken has defrosted, so she cleans and seasons it before placing it in the oven. She grabs two pots form the cabinet, pulls out some broccoli and corn on the cob from the freezer and places them in the pots.

While the chicken is cooking, she goes upstairs and changes into sweat pants and a shirt. Grabbing her laptop, she goes and sits on the bed, but before she settles onto it, she calls her husband, John. She wants to know what time is he coming home, because he always forgets to tell her if he's working late. And she wanted to tell him about her day.

"I know I forgot to call you," he says as soon as he answers the phone. "I'm at Lowe's pricing out material for this possible side job."

"Yeah, yeah, I know…just like the last time."

"I'm sorry. I'll try harder."

"Ok, but I want to tell you something when you get home." She tells him what's she's cooking for dinner, then they hang up. The phone starts to ring as she gets onto her laptop, but she ignores it and logs onto her church's website to see if the weekly Bible study lesson has been posted yet. When she finishes on the website, she grabs the phone again to retrieve the message, only to hear a woman's distant voice on the other end.

Immediately, Sheila thinks that perhaps John's phone has accidentally pocket-dialed her number while he's at Lowe's. But as she continues to listen, she hears the woman's voice fade in and out until finally Sheila hears her say, "John, you don't know what you want."

"You know what I want, I want you," she hears the unmistakable voice of her husband say to the woman.

Hearing those words, and the way he said them, shocks Sheila to the core as tears began to fall down her face. She had been clueless to John's cheating; now, the world as she had known it is crashing to end.

Sheila is devastated. The message has ended, but she still holds the phone to her ear as a thousand thoughts rush through her mind: *Who is this chick? Where did he meet her? How long has this been going on?*

With her mind racing, the tears continue to flow and she starts to wonder if there had been any warning signs. Why didn't she see this coming? But the most important question running through her mind is, *what do I do now?*

She sits up in bed and leans her head against the pillow as she replays the message. *How could he do this to me?* Her mind sorts through the snapshots of their life's events, and she begins to evaluate their marriage. She had already been feeling excluded from his life, but she can't figure out what happened to have brought them to the point of an affair.

Sheila tries to think about what to do, but her mind is too cloudy as all her feelings of hurt, anger, and most of all fear rises to the surface. She can't stop herself from crying as she attempts to comprehend and digest her newfound information. She thinks again about telling him what she knows but decides against it; she is now a private investigator, so she will do some investigating on her own first. In the meanwhile, she will have to stuff down and swallow everything she just learned, and try to figure out how to save this message on her cell phone.

She begins to smell something and finally remembers that she was cooking. She goes downstairs, checks on the chicken and completes the rest of the meal. But she's no longer hungry, so she cleans up and puts the food away. She doesn't even bother to put a plate away for John.

As she checks the time on her cell phone, she realizes it's 9:00 pm and John is still not home. It's just as well, she decides, because she's not sure of what she would do if he were to come home right now.

Sheila goes upstairs. She doesn't even take a shower, but just changes her clothes and gets into bed. She can't even find the words to pray, her feelings are so raw with hurt. She just hopes she will be asleep, or at least in bed pretending to be, when John comes home.

When he does finally come home, John is glad that there are no signs of activity. He hadn't been looking forward to Sheila's nagging and complaining, only some peace and quiet.

John had gotten himself so caught up into Jasmine Anderson that she's all he thinks about now. She's the next-door neighbor to a home where he and his two workers had been doing a job for over a month, thanks to the wife who kept adding on projects for them to do.

As a supervisor at his regular job, John is not always doing hard labor like the men and women he supervises—which allows his time to leave the work site to go check up on his guys on his personal job site. He picks them up early in the morning before he goes to his 7-3 job. When he gets off he goes right to his side job, checking their work and joining them in working.

Jasmine, a single mother with a 5-year-old daughter named Jacqueline, is a woman with a nasty attitude who isn't afraid to speak her mind and will tell anyone off in a minute. Unlike Sheila, a sweet, easygoing, woman that any man would bring home to Mama, Jasmine, on the other hand, is more like the kind of woman that you would occasionally bring around to Mama hoping that she might grow on her over time.

John and Jasmine had seen each other from time to time, but had never really spoken except to say, "Good morning" or "How are you doing?" The day John did meet her, he was pulling up to the house in his big work truck at the same time Jasmine was backing out of her driveway, with Jacqueline in the back seat. After they narrowly avoided a crash, Jasmine jumped out of her car, ready to tell him off.

John got out of his truck, introduced himself, immediately apologized, and asked if they were okay. "Yes, I'm Jasmine and I also apologize," she said, calming down after John introduced himself.

Since the day that John first learned her name, he couldn't stop thinking about this firecracker of a woman who has made a great impression on him. And each time he saw her after that, he tried engaged her in conversation until one day he finally asked her out.

That had been four months ago, and now John feels real good about Jasmine. *I'm really feeling her,* he thinks to himself as he sits on the living room couch, smiling. He would never have thought that he would be having feelings for another woman, especially a younger woman, but it was her fire that intrigued him first and then it was her beauty.

He remembered watching her first and saw that she leaves the house around the same time every morning. He decided to leave her neighbor's house the same time so they would have no choice but to speak to each other. Jasmine's house is not like his. She doesn't live in a single-family house, but a row home with a private driveway and street parking on a nice-sized block, with row houses on both sides of the street.

He snaps out of his thoughts and calls her before it gets too late. He tells her how much he enjoyed their time together that night. He even takes her back to the time they first met by telling her how she almost intimidated him by the way she hopped out of her car and proceeded to tell him off. "For minute I thought I was in the hood the way you came at me," he laughs before adding, "but I can't wait to spend time with you again tomorrow."

Jasmine is also caught up in her feelings for John, and is very excited about their new relationship. They have spent most of their time talking on the phone. But it's been a lot different for Jasmine, who's accustomed to throwing herself into relationships so that, by the fourth month of dating, she would have already slept with them several times. John, however, is the oldest man she's ever dated and he makes her feel alive. They have some deep conversations about their past relationships. They've admitted some of their pet peeves and even shared an embarrassing moment. They've talked about current events, their family lives, whether they're an only child or how many siblings they have. They've even shared their dreams and hopes. John is so easy to talk with and he has a great personality. He seems more laid back than the guys she's used to dating. He doesn't make her feel inadequate or less than a person because she doesn't have a high paying job like he does or isn't informed on certain things like he is. But he educates her in a way as if he's telling her a story on things that she otherwise would have no interest in. He just treats her real nice and he usually calls her at night. There is something about him that just does it for her, and she doesn't want to mess anything up. She had already peeked to see that he didn't have a wedding band on his hand, and therefore, she took it to mean that he wasn't married and maybe had never been married. She never asked him, but just assumed that if he was he would have told her before they got too far.

So for now, she tries to coattail her feelings and follow his lead for the first time in her life. She wants a man of her own, one who will accept her for who she is, including her flaws. In the short time that they've known each other, he's made her want more out of life and want to be a better person. John has even talked to her daughter, Jacqueline, numerous times. To her surprise, Jacqueline really likes him. Sometimes when he calls on the weekends, she allows her to talk to him for a few minutes depending on what time he calls. She likes to keep Jacqueline on a schedule even on the weekends, which makes things much easier when everything stays consistent. But when he calls and Jacqueline knows that Jasmine is talking to him, she'll often ask to talk to him. There are times when she walks away with the phone, and Jasmine can hear her laughing and telling him what she did that day at kindergarten class. Once, Jacqueline recited the entire alphabet to John and then started counting to ten. She told him a couple of names of colors she knows, and even told on some of her classmates to him, like how Mary wasn't sharing her dolls when they had share time. It was like sometimes when he called her he had to have a child's conversation and an adult conversation, and Jasmine often found herself apologizing to him. She didn't know whether he was just being polite or really didn't mind, but John would always tell her that it was okay and not to worry about it. And that made Jasmine feel a closer connection to him.

TWO

John wakes up and looks over at Sheila. She's still sleeping, but his mind is already on seeing Jasmine. He feels no guilt, because he blames Sheila for the affair. She's not fulfilling his needs anymore and all she does is nag and complain.

He gets out of bed slowly, turns to make sure he doesn't wake her, and then heads into the bathroom to take a shower. After hanging up with Jasmine the night before, he had selected his clothes for the next day, ironing and laying them out in the spare bedroom while Sheila slept.

After exiting the shower, he puts on deodorant and lotions himself down. He opens his armoire and pulls out underwear, a tee shirt and socks, then puts it all on before grabbing his sneaker-type shoes and heads into the spare bedroom to get dressed. He had already thought to place his watch, keys and wallet in the room the night before. After he's completely dressed, he sprays on a light mist of cologne and leaves the house.

Sheila had opened her eyes when she felt John get out of the bed, and lay facing the window. So, he thought she was still asleep. As she heard him enter the bathroom, she turned over to see what time it was: 7:30 am on Saturday. She turned back over a few minutes before John came out of the bathroom. She lay there with her eyes closed, listening to him move around the room until he finally left. She strained to hear what he was doing, until 15 minutes later she heard the front door chime. She jumped out of bed and rushed to the window. Peeking through the blinds, she watched him approach his truck before he got in and pulled off.

Now, she turns and gets back into bed. Her tears once again begin to fall until she cries herself back to sleep. She's awoken again by her cell phone ringing. As she grabs it, she realizes the time is now 9:45 am. She answers the phone to hear Traci Carter, one of her church girlfriend.

Traci is a 33-year-old educated woman who teaches at a private school in Fox Chase. She and her husband, Minister Steven Carter, 35, who is a bank manager, have been married for seven years, and they have a five-year old son, Steven, Jr. Traci and Steven had gone through some rough marriage battles of their own, and had almost divorced because of Traci's past as a dancer in a gentleman's club. She had danced her way through college, which paid the bills. She had just started working when she met Steven, where they hit it off after meeting at the laundromat. They had gone through some intense marital sessions with their pastor and first lady, Larry and Patricia Campbell of the Divine Praise Baptist Church, where they been members for about four years. And in their second year of marriage, Steven answered God's call to become an ordained minister himself.

Sheila is a part of the church's new members team. She makes calls to encourage the new members to come out to the church service, which was how Sheila met Traci and became friends. John and Steven also knew each other, and they had all gone out together a few times.

Today, Traci calls to invite Sheila to lunch.

Sheila's trying to get out of it, but Traci isn't taking her excuses. Sheila finally agrees to the time and place to meet her and they hang up. She lays in bed for another 15 minutes before getting up to take a shower, letting the hot water soothe her body as she begins to relax. After showering, she looks for something to wear. She doesn't really want to go out; all she wants to do is stay in bed all day, but she pulls out a lightweight pair of jeans and a shirt. She goes into the spare bedroom to iron them, then gets dressed and makes the bed.

Normally, after Sheila says her prayers she makes her bed and then takes her shower. But she's not herself today and her mind is still cloudy. She takes out her thermal curlers and does her hair. Sheila is an attractive woman with a nice shape in a small frame, and wears her hair in a short cut that flatters her face. She gets her fair share of head turns, which is flattering to her, but the only head she wants to turn is John's—and now he's cheating on her.

While finishing her hair, she glances at the clock and realizes that she's late for lunch. She grabs her purse and hurries down the stairs and out the door.

She gets into her car and drives towards Ruby Tuesday's, which is about 25 minutes away. She arrives ten minutes late.

Traci is already there, seated at a table. After they greet each other, Traci goes on about how she ran into a guy who was a patron at the club she used to dance at. Traci also has a great body; even after having a baby she still looks shapely. Traci tells Sheila about this guy who she thought was stalking her because he followed her to the market and then she recognize him when he first approached her, as the guy who always requested her for a lap dance and was a good tipper. He told her how he'd asked about her at the club, and he always wondered how she's doing and what she's doing now. Traci starts telling Sheila how uncomfortable he made her feel.

"Oh, yeah," is Sheila's response.

Traci stops talking and looks at her. "Ok, girl, what's wrong with you? Is everything ok? You seem to be here but you're not here. So talk to me, tell me what's going on."

"Oh girl, I'll be all right."

But Traci can see Sheila's eyes welling up with tears. "No, you're not all right. What's wrong?" Sheila tries to keep her composure and tells her what's happening.

Traci is so caught off guard by the news that she just sits there for a moment before responding. "I'm so sorry you have to go through this," she finally says. "I'm here for you."

"I don't even know what happened, where things went wrong," Sheila says, dazed, as tears fall from her face. "This is the last thing I would have ever thought John would have done to me."

Traci comforts her friend by getting up to give her a hug. "What you going to do?"

"I don't know…I'm so confused," Sheila answers. "I'm not sure if I should tell him or wait and do some investigating myself."

John comes home after spending the day with Jasmine. Sheila is home, sitting in bed with her laptop, so he speaks to her and heads into the bathroom to take a shower. For John, there's nothing to it to come home and go about his normal routine, which is to take a shower and then head into the basement to relax. Regardless of how many times Sheila tries to spend some time with him, he has little interaction with Sheila and it's almost as if she doesn't exist.

Sheila still has not told John that she knows about his affair. It's been three weeks now, and she's still having a hard time wrapping her head around it. As John walks around as if nothing is going on, Sheila is beginning to think that he has no emotions and that he really doesn't care for her or her feelings. She grieves for the child she will never have with him.

Coming out of the shower, he goes into the bedroom where Sheila is still sitting. Sheila notices that he's wearing a towel. It's not the first time he's done it recently, although he never used to do it before. He barely speaks to her now, making her feel as if they've had some kind of an argument. So Sheila now doesn't know how to approach him without giving what she knows away. There are times that she likes it when he's not around, because she's more relaxed. But on nights like tonight when he's home, she feels tense and hurt because she longs for his attention. Sheila's been longing for John to confess his discrepancies in a sorrowful manner and ask for her forgiveness, but she knows that that's just a dream, not reality. She stares at John, whose back is to her while he's putting on his underwear.

Before John came out of the bathroom, he made sure to wrap a towel around himself in case Sheila was still in the room. She's still in bed using her laptop when he comes out, so he sits in the corner chair to lotion himself. He turns his back toward her when he puts his underwear on and grabs a pair of ball shorts from a dresser drawer. He tries to avoid eye contact with her because he doesn't have anything to say and hopes that she doesn't, either, because he knows that all she'll do is start nagging. He just wants to hurry up, get away from her, and go into the basement so he can relax. There are many times when he falls asleep down there. Sometimes if he wakes up he goes upstairs to bed.

John's feelings for Jasmine are steadily increasing as his feelings for Sheila are steadily decreasing. He thinks that he should somehow feel guilty, but he can't control how his heart feels. He still views Sheila as a good woman with a kind heart and a giving spirit, a real nice, sweet person. But things have changed in their relationship, and now he feels that she's not right for him.

John goes downstairs to his man cave, where he has everything he needs: a 60-inch flat screen HDTV with surround sound, a full bathroom, and a full-size refrigerator. From time to time, he might buy a case of Grey Goose and put a few in the refrigerator. He also has a Lazy Boy reclining chair and a sectional couch. Yeah, he's set.

John calls Jasmine to tell her once again how he

enjoyed being with her all day. They talk for a few minutes and hang up.

The next day, Sheila wakes up to find that John has slept downstairs again.

It's been three weeks since she found out about his affair, and the pain is now unbearable. In the past three weeks, she has experienced every emotion and reaction possible, from snapping, hollering and crying to depression, anger and silence, and it's begun to take a toll on her. She feels as if her life is now one big roller coaster ride and she does not know how to get off.

It's Sunday, and though she wants to pull the covers up over her head and stay in bed, she has a meeting she has to attend. So she gets up, makes the bed, and says a quick prayer before she heads in the bathroom to take a shower. Ten minutes later, she's out of the bathroom and begins her process of getting ready for church. While the shower helps relax her tense muscles, her insides are still a total wreck.

As she gets dressed, she hears John moving around the living room. Her hearts beats faster as she wonders if he's coming up to get ready to go out. She finishes getting ready and gives one last glance in the mirror before going downstairs, where she sees John sitting on the couch. The sight of him makes her heart skip a beat at the same time it breaks even more. John is a very sexy man, and he knows how to dress. He is a little bit taller than her. And God has blessed him with good looks.

He looks up at her. "Hey, I see you're going to church."

"Yeah," is all she manages to say as she reaches the last step.

"You look nice." She makes a mental note of that too, for he always used to tell her how good she looked. Now, it's just "nice." "Thanks."

"I'll be home all day," he says as she opens the front door. "I'm going to fix dinner for you," he calls after her. She says ok before closing the door, but she's not sure if he's heard her.

Sheila can't get in her car fast enough before a tear falls. She starts the car and pulls off without even letting it warm up. She wonders why he's staying home, and to top it off why he's going to cook. "Maybe he's feeling guilty…or does he have a change of heart?" she wonders out loud. Now she's more confused than ever.

She pulls into the church parking lot and finds a spot. It's getting harder to keep pretending everything is fine, so she sits in the car for a few minutes to get herself together. As she reaches the church steps, she takes a deep breath. She asks the Lord for strength to make it through the service, and to please send someone she can talk to who knows and understands. She goes up the steps and pulls open the outer doors to the vestibule, then runs smack into First Lady Patricia Campbell as she opens the sanctuary door.

Sheila greets her with a hug. Lady Campbell hugs her back and whispers in her ear, "You *will* get through this." Sheila stiffens and tries to keep more tears from forming. Lady Campbell lets go and looks at her. "Sister Sheila, you have been so heavy on my mind. I want to see you this week, so call the office and set it up. We really need to talk."

"Ok." Sheila turns to walk away but Lady Campbell grabs her arm. "No, Sheila, I mean it. Set it up for this week." Sheila's nervous now, because she's not sure what Lady Campbell wants. She tries to think of what it could be, until it dawns on her that she could be the answer to the prayer she just prayed. *Well, there's nobody better than Lady Campbell*, she thinks. Driving home from church, Sheila has mixed feelings about what Lady Campbell would say to her.

When she opens the front door, the smell of food greets her and leads her right into the kitchen. John has made smothered pork chops with onions and green peppers, rice and gravy, green beans and apple corn bread muffins. Sheila just stands there, her mouth open. She feels like crying, because it's been years since John has cooked for her. He's cooked for her numerous times since they've been married, but hasn't done it in the last few years. *Why now, why today?* She wonders. *Maybe this is a guilty dinner.*

Grinning, John gives her a kiss on the lips. "I did this because we've been off these last three weeks, and I want to break the tension between us," he says. "Go get out of your church clothes. I'll keep the food warm and make your plate."

Sheila is weakening for him as she goes upstairs to change and wash her hands. As she returns downstairs, she sees John has the dining room table set with candles lit. He pulls out her chair, and they even manage a light conversation while they eat. After eating, he tells her to go upstairs and relax while he cleans up.

Now Sheila is losing all self-control as she goes upstairs to take a shower, trying to clear her head. She gets in bed to watch TV. When John finishes cleaning the kitchen, he also comes upstairs and takes a shower. To Sheila's surprise, he comes out of the bathroom towel less. He lotions himself down, and asks her what she's watching as he puts on his underwear and climbs in the bed.

"What are you doing?" Sheila asks, stunned.

"What it looks like…I'm getting in the bed," he answers as he eases over closer to her. She doesn't know how to react; her emotions are off the chart as her body grows hot.

John attempts to talk to her but she only gives him short answers. Suddenly, he grabs her into his arms. She resists at first, then relaxes and, forgetting everything, enjoys the moment in his arms. She's missed being with him like this. Before she knows it, he's turned her face towards him with his hand and kisses her. To her surprise, she finds herself kissing him back. She longs for him and his touch, so she takes his hand and places it on her breast. He goes back and forth foundling one breast and then the other while kissing her, causing her to moan and arch her back in response to his touch. As their level of passion escalates, what little clothing they have on is soon on the floor. He enters her, and she willingly receives him as they go at it, wildly and desperately clinging to and exploring each other. An hour later, they're still laying together, their bodies intertwined as they sleep.

Sheila awakens on Monday morning, feeling relaxed and satisfied. She turns over to see that John has left for work already. Still feeling foggy and confused, she begins to have mixed feelings about the night before. *What did I do?* she asks herself. *How did I allow this to happen? Was I just dreaming?* Her body is sore as she moves to get up, making her dream a reality. She gets out of bed and makes her way into the bathroom, where she takes a long, hot shower to relax her muscles before preparing for work.

A couple hours after arriving at the office, Sheila calls the church office and schedules an appointment with Lady Campbell for Wednesday at 1:00.

As she wakes up Wednesday morning, Sheila decides to call out from work because her mind is on talking to Lady Campbell about her marriage. She spends the morning lost in her thoughts. By 11:00, she showers and slowly prepares for her meeting. She lives half an hour away from the church, so she leaves home at 12:30. When she arrives, she's a bundle of nerves. Sister Rose, the church secretary, is at her desk, and Sheila goes to the restroom before she approaches Rose. In the restroom, she tries to calm herself down but to no avail.

She greets Sister Rose, who tells her Lady Campbell is waiting for her. As Sheila goes into the office, Lady Campbell gets up and comes around her desk to greet Sheila with a hug. She gestures for Sheila to sit on the couch as she does the same.

"Before we get started, let's pray," she says, and she begins to pray. When she's finished, she asks Sheila how she's been. "I've been praying for you. The Lord had laid you heavy on my heart."

"Well, my job is great...it's my marriage that's not," Sheila says.

"Who, or what, has changed in your marriage?" Lady Campbell asks.

Sheila puts her head down and slowly answers. "I found out through a voicemail message that John is cheating on me."

"Are you sure what you heard was him cheating?"

"I heard him talking to this woman. After she told him that he didn't know what he wanted he said, 'You know what I want, I want you.'" Sheila's tears freely begin to fall. Lady Campbell hands her some tissues and hugs her. She tells her to let it out, and that's just what Sheila does as she cries in her arms. Once Sheila's gotten herself together, they have a long, heart-to-heart talk.

Sheila tells her that John doesn't know that she heard him. She also tells her that he's sleeping more and more in the basement, how she never saw this coming, and how she wanted to have their child. Sheila tells her how she feels so confused and emotionally unstable, and that she wants to use her professional training to investigate some things on her own. Lady Campbell advises her not to do that because she'll probably end up more hurt.

"Early in my marriage, before Pastor became a pastor, he cheated on me," Lady Campbell says. She had been devastated and lost in an array of emotions. She shares with Sheila how she felt it was her fault, wondering how she could have done things differently, and how that changed her and she became so angry. She became obsessed to the point where she started following him, because it was rumored that he was taking up time with a woman from the church. "Now that was a rumor I wanted to see if there was some truth to, so I started to question his whereabouts. His answers were not enough, and I had started to feel insecure within our relationship and within myself. I started watching the women at church to see how they interacted with him, see whether they were too friendly. When I couldn't pinpoint anyone I resorted to following him. The second week, I saw him with her. The first time it was on a Tuesday and he met her at a restaurant after his ministers' meeting. They met in the next town and he greeted her with a kiss on the lips as they sat at a far corner table, looking nice and cozy together. The second time he went to her house, I waited for about an hour. By the time he came back out, I done went through so many emotions and went back to being angry. Girl, I lost it, and all my religion too, when I saw them come out of the house all hugged up and kissing by his car. I snapped, and I got out of my car and confronted them. I asked what was going on here. I looked at him with tears in my eyes and I was full of rage and I asked him what he's doing with her. I told him I had sat out there for about an hour so I demanded that he tell me what he could possibly be doing with her. They both just stood there in shock. Then Larry said, 'Oh baby, I can explain.' Before I knew it, I had reached over Larry and punched this woman in her face, and I was going for him too when he grabbed my fist and pulled me back. The woman had fallen and hollered out in shock. And at first, I still hadn't realized that I had hit her. Larry was hollering at me, telling me to go home and that he would meet me there. Now, I was not about to leave him there with her. And that's when I cursed them both out. I got into his car telling him he better get in now and take me to my car. And he did what I told him to do, leaving this woman standing there stunned in the middle of her driveway. That night we talked, hollered, and cried together. I really struggled in trusting him."

Lady Campbell admits how she was arrested for endangerment because she tried to run down the other woman with her car. "I just wanted to let her know that he was mine and he was no longer available to her or anyone else. She had me arrested but later dropped the charges. And I believe Larry had something to do with it. Oh, Sheila, you don't want to end up like me. For many years, even after we got married, I was known as the 'run you down' pastor's wife."

"I didn't know all this," Sheila says. "But how did y'all make it?"

"If it's God-ordained, what's meant to be will be. Plus, it takes a lot of prayer, fasting and some good Christian counseling."

"How do you know when it's God-ordained?" Sheila asks.

"First, God has the final say. And even, despite everything, if you both truly still love each other and you're both willing to work towards making the wrongs right."

Sheila puts her head down. "I think it's done. But John surprised me on Sunday when I came home from church. He had a romantic dinner prepared and somehow, we ended up kissing and we made love. But now he acts like it was nothing, so now I believe that John doesn't love me anymore. I think she stole him away from me."

"Right now, you need to focus on yourself before you have a nervous breakdown," Lady Campbell says, and tells her she can come and see her anytime she wants for counseling.

THREE

Today's the day Sheila gets her chance to take on her own case at work. She's nervous, yet confident that she'll do well.

Mr. Gilford gives her a case that involves a mother who believes that her children are doing unlawful things. Ronnie, the receptionist, has scheduled Sheila's interview with Ms. Amanda Green for 10:00 am, and it's now 9:30. So Sheila stocks the conference room with water, coffee and danishes, then she returns to her office to wait.

At 9:50, Ronnie buzzes Sheila's office. "Your 10:00, Ms. Amanda, is here."

"Thank you, I'll be out in a minute," Sheila answers. She stands up, takes a breath, and says a quick prayer.

At first glance, Amanda's appearance seems to be conservative yet wholesome. Her clothes are slightly out of style but well kept. Her hairstyle makes her look older than Sheila believes she is. Sheila takes one last breath as she extends her hand to greet Amanda and leads her to the conference room, where they sit down at the table. Sheila has a pad and pen ready to take down some information. "What brings you here today?" Sheila begins.

Now it's Amanda who takes a breath. "I'm a single mother of two teenagers, and I believe that they are into all sorts of things," she answers. "You see, I have a boy and a girl and I think they're doing drugs because of the change in their behaviors and attitudes." She pauses, then continues by saying that her children, for the most part, are good and that they've never been any real trouble. "But I'm now afraid that they will soon get into trouble if their attitudes don't change. I just want to know what I'm dealing with so I can try to figure out how to handle them."

Sheila asks for their photos and Amanda hands them to her. "These are two years old, but the kids look just about the same."

Sheila studies the photos. "Tell me about your children the things you know."

Amanda begins by naming the school they attend and their friends she knows about and where they live. She also tells Sheila where she believes they still hang out at. "I have enough to get started with," Sheila says. She verifies Amanda's contact information and asks her if she has any questions.

"Yeah, how soon will you be starting? What are

you going to do?"

"I'll be starting tomorrow morning. What time do they leave for school, and are you home when they leave?"

"Yes, I am," Amanda says, "and they leave at 7:00."

"Good, I'll be doing my surveillance around 6:30." Sheila stands up and she extends her hand to Amanda, who also gets up. "I'll be in touch with you soon." She directs her to see Ronnie to pay the retainer fee and other expenses.

Sheila goes back to her office, plops in her chair and smiles, for she not only feels confident in herself but glad that Ms. Amanda also seems to feel confident in her abilities.

Meanwhile, Amanda sits in her car outside, wondering if she's doing the right thing. Although she trusts Sheila, she wants her kids to have an open and trusting relationship where they can come and talk with her about anything.

Sheila sits in her car across the street from Amanda's house, her camera in hand. She's waiting to snap some pictures of Amanda's kids when they come outside.

The front door opens and the kids come out. Sheila quickly takes some shots, thinking they look like two harmless kids. They walk in front of her car, not even noticing her. She follows them as they meet up with two other kids. One is smoking and Amanda's son takes a puff. They all walk to school, lingering outside the building until the bell rings and they go inside.

Sheila leaves and returns half an hour before

school lets out that afternoon. She finds a spot where she can see the front door. The school bell rings, and five minutes later the students come pouring out. Sheila focuses on the crowds of kids until she finally spots Amanda's children. Her daughter is hanging all over a boy, and Sheila takes a picture of them kissing. As her brother and his friends walk away from the school, one of them light up what appears to be a joint. The girl and her friends eventually start walking and catch up with her brother and his friends.

They all head into an old, abandoned building. Sheila slowly goes in after them, tiptoeing further into the space. She doesn't see anyone but she can hear their voices. She sees a set of steps and slowly eases her way upstairs, where she spots the kids in the far-left corner of a room, sitting on a couple of mattresses and getting high. For two hours, they get turned up to the point of becoming loud and destructive, and finally begin trashing the place. On their way home, they smash a few car windows and even slash some tires, laughing the whole time.

Sheila takes pictures of that, as well. When the kids arrive home, they all go inside. For the next hour, Sheila stays parked out front until the other kids leave. After they leave, she waits another 15 minutes before she finally pulls off.

Sheila follows them four other times. The last time, she discovers the children after school smoking in an abandoned building, but this time they also go to the local shopping center and both do some shoplifting. She manages to catch a snapshot of them both stealing small items; this time, they aren't caught. As she follows them out the store, they start laughing and go home. The girl has stolen make-up, candy bars and underwear, while her brother has stolen underwear and socks.

Sheila thinks it's just a matter of time before they get caught. She leaves the store and goes to the office. When she gets there, she hands the films to Ronnie, the receptionist, to have them developed, and compiles her notes so Ronnie can type them up. Three days later, Ronnie gives her the developed film along with her notes. Sheila asks her to please schedule a meeting with Ms. Amanda.

Sheila meets Amanda to go over her findings. Amanda appears to be nervous, so Sheila tries to reassure her by saying everything will be all right. She hands her the photos, which are arranged in date order.

Sheila explains each photo and expresses her concerns about a few, like the photos of the kids shoplifting. "If they had been caught and arrested, there could have been charges pressed against them. That also applies for these photos of vandalism to the warehouse, and these of them slashing those car tires. There would have been some serious charges against them and they would have needed a good lawyer." Amanda sits there in somewhat shock at her kids' behavior. She can no longer hold in her emotions and she cries. "I don't understand. They're good kids."

"I don't have any kids, but I have no doubt that they're good kids. But they're teenagers who have too much free time on their hands, which is making them bored. And their friends are having a great influence on them," Sheila says. "They need a job and some responsibilities. Do they do chores?"

"Very little, and they half do them," Amanda answers.

"So, if they have less time to spend with their friends, the better off they'll be."

"Thank you. I appreciate all your help and your truthfulness. And you're right…they do have too much time on their hands. So, I will be taking your advice and they will be getting a job."

Sheila smiles. "That's the way to do it. You take charge of your family. Is there anything else I can do for you?"

"No, thank you for everything."

"I'm glad to have been of help to you. And if you should need me again don't hesitate to call me," Sheila says as they get up.

"Ok, I won't," Amanda says. She walks to the door and leaves.

Sheila sits back down and writes her case notes conclusion: *Client saw photos and agreed that her children need to find jobs and take on some responsibilities. Client also states if further help is needed she will call. Case closed.* Sheila comes out of her office and hands Amanda's file to Ronnie, the receptionist. She suddenly grabs her mouth in pain. "What, your tooth again?" Ronnie says. "I told you, you need to have it looked at."

"Yeah, I know," Sheila says. "I'm going to make an appointment now." A few minutes later she comes out and tells her they have an opening in half an hour, so she's leaving for the day.

At the dentist, she's greeted by the receptionist, Jasmine, who says, "I haven't seen you in a while. How are you?"

Sheila says, "I would be doing better if my tooth wasn't hurting."

"We'll take good care of you. You can have a seat and we'll be right with you."

"Ok girl, and maybe I can catch up with you later after my mouth stops hurting." When Sheila comes out from seeing the dentist 35 minutes later, she's feeling no pain. She had lost a filling and he refilled it, so now she's good. Her mouth is numb, but she has no pain.

She pays Jasmine and they chat for a while. Jasmine tells her about the changes that's being done there at the office and how she feels that they might be getting rid of her soon. She asks Sheila if they need a receptionist in the office where she works, or if she knows of anyone who needs one. She takes one of the dentist's cards, writes her number on it, and gives it to Sheila. Sheila hands her one of her own cards before she leaves.

When Sheila comes home from the dentist, to her surprise she sees John's truck in the driveway. Being around him is torturing her, because she's so confused and doesn't understand why she still wants him sexually, especially after their last encounter, and especially knowing what he did. She doesn't feel desperate, but wanting to hold onto her marriage makes her feel a little desperate—especially when she hasn't let on that she knows about his affair.

As she enters the house, she doesn't see him on the first floor so she figures he's in the basement. She goes upstairs, gets out of her clothes and takes a shower. And after putting on her nightgown. She goes back downstairs to make something light to eat, for her mouth is still a little numb even though she feels no pain. She decides to make a sandwich and has sat down at the table to eat it when John appears from the basement.

"Is everything ok? You're home so early."

"Yeah, but I just left the dentist. I needed a tooth refilled. So why are you home?"

"The guys are finishing up on a job and I decided to come home from a little bit," John answers. Sheila thinks this is the most they've talked in a while. Her heart aches and longs for what they once had.

John makes a sandwich and sits down with her to eat. They're silent at first, until John asks, "How's your mouth? Is it still numb?"

"A little numb, but I feel no pain." Sheila wants to say more but the pain in her heart won't allow her. She just wants to hurry up and finish eating, so she gets up.

"Where are you going?"

"I'm going to clean up, then I'm going upstairs."

"Ok." I'll be up."

Stop with all this, she wants to tell him. *What are you doing? I know about your affair so how long are you going to continue to play this game with me?* Instead, she just looks at him silently and proceeds to clean up.

Sheila walks into her room, she grabs a book and gets into bed to read. She starts reading but she can't focus, so she puts the book down and grabs her laptop, trying to find something before John comes upstairs. All she can do is try to keep busy or at least look like it, when he comes upstairs. She's nervous yet excited. She hears him coming just as she get on the Internet, so she click on a headline article about Jay-Z and Beyonce's sister. As John enters the room, she peeks up at him but says nothing.

John sees her in bed on her laptop. "Is your mouth still numb?"

Without looking directly at him, Sheila looks up. " No, it's fine now."

"That's good. What are you looking at?"

"What? Oh, I'm just looking at the headline news right now."

John sits on the bed and leans over to see the screen and the photos of Jay-Z and Beyonce's sister. "Wow, isn't that crazy? What do you think?"

"Yeah, but it's hard to tell what's really going on. Nobody's talking."

"Yeah, I know, but it looks serious."

Sheila cuts her eye in his direction. *Really? Is this all you have to say to me?* She thinks. *How about you tell me the truth about how you're cheating on me, and you're sorry and it won't happen again? How about you tell me the you still love me and you really want to work on us? What about that, John, I don't want to talk about no Jay-Z.* She feels like she's going to choke because the words are trying to come out, but she hold her tongue.

John gets up and messes around in the room for a little while. He takes out his shaving kit and goes in the bathroom to shave, which takes him a good 25 minutes. Then he closes the door and takes a shower, which takes him another 15 to 20 minutes. When he finally comes out, he has a towel wrapped around him. He puts on some lotion, then goes to his dresser and pulls out socks, an undershirt, and underwear. He puts them on and goes to his closet and pulls out a pair of jeans and a shirt. Once he's fully dressed it's around 4:30. He grabs a pair of sneakers and puts them on and he sits there for a few minutes, looking at Sheila and debating whether he should go and see Jasmine. He loves Sheila, but isn't in love with her. Though he feels bad somewhat, he get up and tells her he's going out.

Sheila can't say a word, so she just nobs her head.

John grabs a few things off his dresser and leave the room. He almost feels Sheila's pain as he head downstairs and hesitates for a second, feeling torn. He knows that it hurts her when he always leaves out and never includes her. But then he thinks about Jasmine and how she makes him feel. And so he leaves.

Sheila is once again brokenhearted and frustrated. She doesn't know how much more she can take. She hears the door close, and like all the other times, she jumps up and goes to the window and watches him leave. She wants to stop doing it, but she can't stop herself. It's as if something pulls her to the window and again, like every other time, she starts to cry. *Why, Lord?* She prays. *Lord, please help me. How much more of this will I have to take? I can't take no more. Please help me.*

FOUR

Jasmine's ex-boyfriend, Paul, calls her because he wants to see his daughter, Jacqueline. He hasn't seen her in about two weeks and he has some things to give her.

Paul and Jasmine's relationship is far better now than it was when they first broke up. Jasmine agreed not to take him to court for child support as long as he continues supporting their child. When they first broke up, Paul would call the house at all hours of the day and night and would always drive by the house. If he saw a car there he didn't recognize, he would go on a jealous rage and accuse her of having a man over, which would lead them into bad arguments. Now, however, they're able to communicate without a lot of arguing, and he's not driving by to check up on them anymore.

Jasmine tells Paul that Jacqueline is at her mom's house. He wonders why she's over there again but simply says ok and doesn't question her. Jacqueline had been at her mother's the last time he had her, but he doesn't say anything. Instead, he asks her how she's doing and if she received the check he sent last week.

"Oh yeah, thanks," she says. "I'm doing ok."

But even if she wasn't, he'd be the last person she would tell.

Jasmine works as a receptionist in a dentist's office. The pay is ok but still not enough to make ends meet, so she uses the money Paul sends to help pay the bills and buy things for Jacqueline.

Paul calls Ms. Anderson, Jasmine's mother. She tells him to pick Jacqueline up at 2:00 and to have her back by 7:00. Paul and Ms. Anderson always got along well. She never got in their business, and when she did it was because either he or Jasmine had pulled her into their stuff. But she never displayed any partial feelings; she would tell them both when either of them was wrong.

As Paul pulls up to Ms. Anderson's house, Jacqueline comes running out, hollering, "Daddy!" He gets on his knees, and she runs into his arms and squeezes his neck as tightly as she can. He picks her up and twirls her around, making her laugh. After putting her down, he gives her a big bag. She squeaks with excitement as she pulls out a Barbie with clothes and a doll house.

Ms. Anderson takes the gifts and gives Jacqueline's jacket to Paul. He puts it on her and they walk to the car. He straps her in the booster seat and they head for the park. Jacqueline's so excited, and she plays with everything on this nice day. Afterwards, he takes her to McDonald's, where she eats a cheeseburger Happy Meal. They talk while they eat, and he asks how she's doing in school.

"I know my ABCs and I can count up to 20 and—oh, I know some colors and shapes!"

"Oh baby, I'm so proud of you. So, does Mom have a man friend?"

She stops eating. "Yeah, like Mr. John. He almost hit us with his truck and Mom talks to him a lot."

"You mean on the phone, right?"

Jacqueline drinks some of her soda. "Yeah, and he comes over the house sometimes too."

He does, does he? Paul stops talking because he's lost in his thoughts, and they finish eating in silence. They drive back to Ms. Anderson's house. He tells Jacqueline he loves her, hugs her and asks if she had a good time.

"Yes, Daddy I had fun! When can we do this again?"

"Soon."

"Ok!" she says, and runs to tell Ms. Anderson everything they did.

"Yeah, we went to the park and she ate McDonald's," Paul says. "She should be tired."

"Ok. I'll give her a bath when we go in. How you been?"

"Well, you know me…I'm doing all right. How about yourself?"

"Besides the little aches and pains, I'm doing all right myself," Ms. Anderson answers.

"I love you and I'll see you later baby girl," Paul says to Jacqueline, and heads to his car.

As Paul drives home, he thinks about another man being around his daughter. It's driving him crazy, and all sorts of thoughts run through his mind. He feels it's too soon for Jasmine to be dating, yet alone bringing some guy around his daughter.

He had moved away after their break up because he was a bit obsessed, but now he just feels that this guy is moving in on Jasmine and could be trying to buy Jacqueline with gifts. He doesn't know how developed their relationship is, but what's really driving him crazy is that Jacqueline likes this guy. This is making Paul feel that he's being replaced.

He drives by Jasmine's house to see what's going on. At first, he just sits in his car, watching the house but seeing nothing. He finally decides to call her and announce that he's close by the area and wants to stop in to see Jacqueline.

Jasmine pauses but agrees and quickly says, "We're not starting this popping up thing?"

"Ok, I know," Paul answers. He waits about five minutes before he gets out of the car, walks up to the house, and rings the bell. Jasmine lets him in and they talk for a few minutes.

"Oh, I see you've painted," Paul says.

"Yeah, I'm trying to fix the place up some. Jacqueline's in her room." He goes upstairs and looks around. He peeks in Jasmine's room and in the bathroom before knocking on his daughter's room.

"Come in." He opens the door. "Daddy!" she hollers, jumping up from her bed and running to him.

He scoops her up and gives her a bear hug as she clings tightly to his neck. He holds her out some to just look at her, to see how she's growing. "Daddy, I didn't know you were coming over!" she says.

"Well, I wanted to surprise you," he says as he kisses her cheek.

"Oh Daddy, this is a surprise!" They sit down to talk.

"I like your room," Paul says, hoping she'll start talking.

"Thank you, Daddy! I picked the color."

"Did Mom paint?"

"No, Mr. John and his men did."

"Who?" Paul says, pretending he's forgotten who John is.

"Daddy I told you, he's Mom's friend. He's working on Mr. and Mrs. Fishers' house next door."

"Oh, ok," Paul says. In his head, he's really wondering about Jasmine's and this guy John's relationship, but he turns his focus back to his daughter. They talk and play around in her room before he leaves.

He gets his last hug and kiss before he gets up. "You know you're Daddy's little princess."

She beams at him. "I know. I love you, Daddy."

"I love you too, Princess." He gets up and leaves, closing her door shut. He stops in the bathroom and checks out the new fixtures. He goes downstairs to Jasmine, unable to contain himself. "Who's this guy John who did all this work?"

"What? He's a friend."

"Yeah. Is he a friend or your boyfriend?"

"Ok, he's my boyfriend."

"You don't think that's too fast, and is he around Jacqueline?"

"No and yes," Jasmine says, "but he will not and can't replace you as her father."

"Oh, no man will ever replace me. I only left seven months ago." "How serious is this, I just don't want Jacqueline getting confused., I'm her father."

Jasmine says, "Yeah Paul, she knows that and you left, so don't try to control things over here."

Paul starts getting mad. "You know what? I better go before I say something wrong."

FIVE

John arrives at Jasmine's house just as she returns home from dropping off her daughter at her mother house. They go inside together. John watches her as she moves about the house. To him, this woman feels so right that he wants her as his own.

Jasmine Anderson is 27 years old and had been in a long-term relationship with her daughter's father, Paul Turner, for 11 years. Though she had her own issues, she just had to get away from Paul with his bad temper and controlling, distrustful ways. Paul was her high school boyfriend, and they had known each other well. They grew up in the same section of town, although she lived in a better part. Her parents were together while he had been raised by his mom. He never knew his father because he died when he was young. Paul didn't have a real male role models other than his two older brothers, so whatever he learned about life and relationships came from his mother, brothers, and of course, the streets.

John follows Jasmine into the kitchen, where she pulls a frying pan out of a cabinet and takes eggs, bacon, and bread to make toast out of the refrigerator. Before starting to cook, she looks over at John and smiles; she's happy that this is the first thing she's cooking for him. After eating, she cleans up and they go into the living room to watch TV. They are still learning about each other, yet they feel so comfortable with each other.

John has already told Jasmine that he's married but they don't share the same bed, and that he sleeps in the basement. According to him, they co-exist together and do their own thing. At first, Jasmine didn't know that John was married because he didn't wear a ring, nor was there a sign that one had been on his finger. So of course, she was taken aback when he finally did tell her, but by that point she had already begun having feelings for him so she chose to believe him.

Now, they snuggle up on the couch in front of the TV, each lost in their own thoughts. *Oh, please God, don't let there be another shoe to drop,* Jasmine thinks. *Let him be the man of my dreams.*

Wow, this woman has really gotten into my head, John thinks. *Now I'm confused about my feelings for her and my wife.*

"How is the work coming along next door?" Jasmine asks, breaking the silence.

John loves to talk about his work, so he tells her they just finished installing the jet tub, and now they have to paint the master bedroom and bathroom and the work will be done. "So far, we've done their master bedroom, bathroom and hallway. We did their kitchen and the only thing left is their basement, unless the wife adds something else."

"Oh, you must feel good when the work is done and the owner's happy and tells you how beautiful everything looks," Jasmine says. "Do you take before and after pictures so you can show off your work?"

"Sounds like you could be my sales and marketing person!"

She laughs. "Yeah, I can even answer the phones for you, for a small fee."

"Oh? And what might that be?"

She looks at him. "Oh…you can do some work around here to make this place look beautiful."

He looks at her, then around the place. "Like what?"

"Well, the kitchen and bathrooms need an update, for starters. And the whole house needs to be repainted. That's all."

"That's all, huh?" he laughed. "Sounds to me like you've really thought about this."

"Well, yeah I have, a little…"

Jasmine is excited, because this is the first time John has come over since he's done all the work in her house. Her mother has Jacqueline for the weekend, and she wants to have the place looking good when he gets there.

Jasmine feels that her relationship with John is really growing and she wants to see him a lot more. He makes her feel warm and fuzzy inside. Tonight is supposed to be special because John said that he would spend the night, so she's extra excited as she anticipates his arrival. She's cooked a dish that he likes and everything is ready; she's just waiting for him.

John is at home, getting ready to go over to Jasmine's, and Sheila is there in the bedroom. He's torn as he takes several quick glances at Sheila while she sits in bed with her laptop. He feels a little tug and almost changes his mind; he's feeling guilty because Sheila is right there, watching him get ready to meet another woman—a woman he now has almost stronger feelings for than he has for his wife. It continues to tear at him, but he continues to get dressed. He never tells Sheila exactly where he's going, but just says that he'll be back later.

"Ok," is all Sheila answers, but what she really wants to say is, *when are WE going out?* But every time she does, he gets mad. She hates watching him leave her.

Once in the car, John breathes a sigh of relief and calls Jasmine to tell her he's on his way. He begins to have mixed feelings as he pulls off, so he tries to justify his actions with his thoughts. *Sheila drives me crazy. She always nagging and complaining about something and she just gets on my nerves. Now that Jasmine has come into my life, I feel alive again and like a new man. I have more energy and I'm excited.* Now he feels better and can't wait to spend time with Jasmine.

He pulls up to the house and parks. Jasmine opens the door as he's getting out of his truck. She's waiting to greet him, and once again he feels that he could get used to coming home to her every night. John walks into the house and Jasmine kisses him passionately. "Are you ready to eat?"

"Yeah, why not?" He walks into the kitchen to wash his hands and then goes into the dining room to see that she's already prepared the table. He sits down while she serves him and they eat. After dinner, he helps her clean up and they go into the living room.

"The food was good," John says as he sits on the couch and looks around. "The color you chose makes the room look brighter and bigger. You have a good eye."

"I told you before that I could be your assistant," Jasmine says. "Now you see it."

"Yeah, I know. This place really looks nice, though. Should we watch TV?" he says as he reaches for the remote. They find a movie and watch it quietly.

When the movie is over, Jasmine asks John if he wants pie and ice cream.

"That sounds good." Jasmine goes into the kitchen to warm up the pie and they eat while they talk. John asks her what's been going on with her and what's the latest regarding her job.

"Well, Jaqueline's dad, Paul, has told me he's concerned about you being around Jaqueline. He asked me how serious our relationship was and said that he didn't want Jaqueline getting confused."

"So, what did you tell him?"

"I told him that he will always be her father and that you were not replacing him."

"And what did he say after that?"

"He said she's young and he just doesn't want her confusing the roles of her father and you as a man I'm seeing, who spends time around her." Jasmine adds, "I think he was ok with things after that. And now to answer your question about my job...it really seems like they might get rid of me so I need to start looking now."

"Well, if you feel that way then you should. Maybe you can ask some of the patients, the ones you feel you can trust who wouldn't mention it to one of the other workers."

"Yeah, I did talk to someone before and we exchanged numbers," Jasmine remembers. "I'll give her a call."

They were quiet for a moment, and then Jasmine moves closer into John's arms. "I'm so glad you're here. Now we can have some real time together."

"Yeah, it does feel good." He kisses her passionately, and they sit there continuing to kiss like two teenagers on her parents' sofa. John grabs her breasts and caresses them both sensually.

Jasmine is now really lost to what she's feeling as John touches her. She doesn't want him to stop; she wants more. She wants him, and not just physically. Then the feeling stops and she opens her eyes to see John looking at her. "Why did you stop? What's wrong?" she asks.

"Nothing's wrong. I don't want to rush. I want to take my time."

"So, does that mean you're spending the night?"

Am I, John thinks. "Yes."

Through her excitement Jasmine hugs him, then they sit and watch another movie.

The movie is over by 9:30, and John and Jasmine are still cozily sitting together. As another show begins, Jasmine finally speaks and asks John if he wants anything to drink.

"No, I'm fine for now." Then he says, out of his own awkward, nervous feelings, "Do you still want me to stay over?"

"Yes, I do, but that's if you want to."

"Sure, I do." He looks deeply into her eyes. "Yeah, I really do." He leans in to kiss her. Jasmine receives his kiss and returns it with a passion of her own, which makes it easier for her to ask him if he's ready to go upstairs now.

Of course, John says yes.

They get up and Jasmine turns off the TV. "I'm going to check the back door."

"Ok, I'll check the front door," John says. As Jasmine walks back into the living room, John has just finished checking the door. She tells him to head to the steps while she turns off the lights. They walk upstairs together, both more nervous than excited and lost in their own expectations.

Walking into her bedroom, John looks around before sitting in the chair that's on the side of the bed. Jasmine turns on her TV to help ease the awkwardness, then playfully pulls him up and leads him to the edge of the bed. She tells him she has strong feelings for him and that she wants this to be the first night of more to come.

John looks at her. "My feelings for you are strong, as well." He hugs and kisses her passionately.

Jasmine breaks free and begins to remove her clothes. She goes into the bathroom and comes out with her bra and panties on. John had removed his clothes except for his underwear, and after she comes out of the bathroom he goes in.

He returns to the room to find her lying in bed, waiting for him. He gets excited upon seeing her, and his manhood rises. He gets in bed next to her and kisses her and then starts to explore her body passionately. Jasmine starts to explore him as well. They kiss, touch and explore each other until they're both satisfied, then lay there in silence, lost in their own thoughts.

This man is everything I ever wanted, Jasmine thinks. *It feels so right.*

John thinks, *Wow, the sex is good. And she appears to fit well with me. So far, we're doing well together.*

After a while, Jasmine rolls closer, lays her head on his chest, and they fall asleep. Around 1:40 am she wakes up. She goes to the bathroom, rinses her mouth out, and goes back to bed.

John feels her movements, and when she comes back he asks if she's ok. He also goes to the bathroom to rinse his mouth, and when he gets back into the bed he spoons her, cups one of her breasts, then turns her over and enters her again. About 45 minutes later, they're both huffing and puffing from pure exhaustion and exhilaration. They both fall back to sleep.

When Jasmine wakes up again, she feels a little sore but good and happy as she lays there, looking at him. John wakes up to her staring at him. "What's that look? Tell me what you're thinking," he says.

"I was studying your face and thinking how handsome you are, and how much I want you as mine completely."

John sits up. "I know you do, baby."

Jasmine takes a shower, then gets a towel and facecloth out for John. "While you take your shower, I'm going to go downstairs and fix some breakfast so you can eat before you leave." John takes his shower, then eats and helps Jasmine clean up. They sit in the living room for a few minutes before he leaves.

Jasmine watches him pull off. So does Paul, who drove by the house last night because he was going to try and pop in to see his daughter. When he saw this John guy's truck, however, he left but came by again and saw it was still there. It's now 9:30 am, and Paul watches him pull off, with Jasmine at the door wearing a robe.

SIX

Traci returns home from lunch with Sheila, feeling stunned by her news. She's also full of concern for her friend and a little for herself. She had been trying not to be that nosey, talkative friend, but a good listener who gave her support and encouragement. As for herself, she's still concerned about the man from the gentleman's club, because she thought he had been following or stalking her before he approached her. Traci hasn't told Steven about it because she feels she could just be overreacting. And, well, the *real* reason she hasn't told Steven is that she had developed some feelings for the guy when she had been a dancer, and she still feels an attraction towards him. He wasn't like the other guys in the club, but is respectful and even somewhat charming. When she danced for him, he engaged her in conversations. For now, Traci decides to let it go; seeing him brings back old feelings and memories.

Steven comes home and Traci can't wait to tell him all that's happening with Sheila and John. "Is she going to tell John that she knows about his affair?" Steven asks.

"Well, she doesn't know yet."

"Wow, that's crazy...I'm sorry to hear that," Steven replies. He tells Traci to just be a good friend and not get caught up in their problems, and then says that he'll be praying for them.

"That's the thing," Traci says. "Even though I don't know John like I know Sheila, I would have never thought of him as being a cheater. And I know how much Sheila loves him and how badly she wants to have his child."

Again, Steven tells her to not get too involved. Traci gives him that "whatever" look. "Yeah, I know."

What she really wants to do is give Sheila some advice and suggest that she talk with First Lady Campbell at church. The first lady had been the one who helped her see things from Steven's perspective. She helped her understand how he felt when men stared at her because of her past as an exotic dancer, and that Steven didn't like the thought that other men were imaging her naked. It's then that Traci realizes how much her past has affected him, and that alone is a good reason to keep things to herself. She feels a little paranoid, and wonders whether it's just that she secretly wants to see the guy from the gentleman's club again. Traci is confused and wants to share her feelings with Sheila, but knows that Sheila has bigger issues than she does right now.

Traci's so caught up in her thoughts that she doesn't hear Steven calling her until he calls her name for the third time. "Yeah?" she finally answers.

"I'm going to the hospital to visit Brother Cook."

"Ok," she calls back, and she hears him leaves. Traci starts to fix dinner but realizes that she's out of green peppers. She calls her next-door neighbor to see if their daughter could come over to stay with Steven Jr. so she can run to the neighborhood market.

When she comes out of the market, she runs right into him—the man from the strip club. They're both surprised. "Wow, hey…do you remember me?" he says. *I can't stop thinking about you,* she says to herself.

"So, what *is* your name?" he asks. "I don't want to call you Cinnamon. My name is Paul."

"What? My name? Oh, my name is Traci."

"Nice to run into you again, Traci. Are you ok? You look a little upset."

"I'm fine," she says. "Just surprised to keep seeing you."

"Oh, I live close by on Delaney Street. Do you live nearby?"

Traci pauses. "Yes, off of Brook and Reed Street."

"Oh, I know where that's at. They're nice houses over there. Have you lived there long?"

"Just five years."

"Yeah, I just moved over here about a month ago and I don't know my way around," he says. "Can you suggest some good restaurants? And where are the hot spots for entertainment?" He sees that look again. "Oh, of course, if you don't mind showing me around if you have the time."

She looks at him and feels her attraction for him rising. "Well, it's just that I'm married with a 5-year-old, and I work."

"So how long have you been married and what type of work do you do?"

"I've been married for seven years and I'm a

teacher at a private school in the Fox Chase area."

"Well, I'm not trying to cause any problems for you," he says, "but it's just that I don't know anybody and I'm familiar with you."

Traci speaks without thinking. "We'll work something out."

Paul is fuming after he leaves Jasmine's house, and he desperately wants a drink. When he gets around his neighborhood he wants to see Traci, so he drives around to some of the places he'd seen her before, hoping to see her again. He wants her opinion. He drives to the market and sits there for a little while, looking for her, before deciding to ride by the mall.

At first, he rides around in the parking lot, then sits in the car with his flashers on by the entrance, waiting, until she comes outside, walking quickly. He honks his horn at her, trying to get her attention. She looks in his direction but she doesn't see him, so he lays on his horn while sticking his head out the window, calling her name. She finally sees him and stops.

He pulls his car up and stops next to her. "Hi. I'm sorry, I don't want to appear to be this stalker guy always showing up, but once again, I don't really know anybody yet and I have a situation with my daughter's mother and wanted to talk to you about it to get a woman's point of view, to help me to understand."

"Oh yeah, ok. What is it?" Traci says.

"If you don't mind, can we go somewhere so we can sit down and have a drink or something? I mean, if you have time, that is."

"Sure," Traci replies, surprising herself with how

quickly she answers.

"Great. Do you know where we should go?"

"Follow me." She drives to a restaurant in the next town. They go in and are seated at a booth in the back.

"Thanks for agreeing to come here," Paul says. "Do you want a meal or some appetizers and drinks?" Paul says to Traci as the waiter comes over.

"Appetizers and drinks are fine," Traci answers. They order two appetizers and drinks.

Traci says, "So what's going on?"

"Well, my ex-girlfriend is seeing this guy who's working on the house next door to her and he's being around my daughter."

"Ok…so, is this about your daughter or your ex?"

"No, I'm not jealous. I've moved on but she doesn't get it. I don't want my 5-year-old confused between my role and this guy's. I'm her father. I don't know how serious their relationship is but he did some work in her house that I know she can't afford."

"Oh, I see," Traci says. "So, you don't want no man around your daughter because she might like him and get attached to him."

"Well yeah, she's too young it will only confuse her, especially if he's buying her gifts. I'm supposed to be the only man right now in her life buying her things. I just don't want her to be confused."

"So, what's your ex saying?"

"Truthfully, she said I was just jealous that she has someone and I'm trying to be controlling. I tried to explain to her it's not like that, it's about my daughter being confused. And my ex wasn't getting that it's not about her, it's about me and my daughter's relationship. And the only thing I have a concern about regarding my ex is will she be bringing every man she's dating around my daughter, that's all. I was over there a little while ago and I left because I was getting mad and I didn't want to say the wrong things and make matters worse."

"Well, that was a smart thing to do," Traci says. "Don't give up. Keep the communication lines open. Y'all will have to compromise in how you co-parent."

"Yeah, you're right. Thank you." Then he says, "So what made you want to teach?"

"Well, I was inspired by my favorite teacher in middle school, Ms. Peterson. She was so cool and she made learning English and history fun and easy."

"Ok. So, you were dancing while you were in college?"

"Yeah. It helped a whole lot."

Paul says, "Look, I'm not going to lie…I had missed you, and then I stopped going there."

"You were nice to me. We had good, interesting conversations while I danced for you. And thanks again for the conversations and the good tips!"

"You're welcome," Paul says. "Being with you now sure got my mind off my situation." They eat and talk for an hour. Before they leave, he asks when she can show him around.

"Let's exchange numbers now and I'll call you soon," Traci says, taking out her cell phone.

Paul asks for and pays the check. "Thank you again," he says as they walk out to their cars.

Traci says, "Well, I must admit I was taken aback when you said you have a daughter."

"Yeah…she's my heart."

"I have to go, but thanks for the food and drinks,"

Traci says. They say good night and he walks over to his car.

Traci drives home thinking about Paul. She hopes he listens to her and keeps communicating with his ex about their daughter. Traci realizes that Paul has taken up space in her mind, and she's enjoying it. They always had good conversations, and now she's learned they both have a 5-year-old child in common. She knows she's wrong for entertaining these thoughts and she shouldn't allow herself to go there, but it's already taken off and she can't control her emotions. Traci is scared because Paul is the first man that she's been attracted to since she's been married, and plus they already have a little history together.

It's been three days since Traci met with Paul, and every day since he has invaded her thoughts.

Paul is 6'3", brown-skinned and well built. He dresses well but he's not flashy. He's a modest, laid back man. Traci has a lighter complexion than Paul, small framed but nicely shaped. She has a short haircut and dresses conservatively. She's also modest and laid back.

Traci is going crazy; she doesn't know how to deal with her developing feelings for Paul. In desperation, she calls Sheila in hopes of doing some catching up and maybe share with her what she's feeling for Paul. "Hey," she says as Sheila answers the phone, "just wanted to catch up. How are you? Can we go out, or maybe I can come over?"

"Oh girl, this is awful. I feel like I'm going crazy," Sheila answers.

"I'm coming over. I'll be there in about 20 minutes."

"Ok," Sheila says. "John just left."

Traci drives over, wondering how she can bring up what's going on with her to Sheila and still be sensitive to Sheila and her own situation. When she gets to her house, Sheila greets her and they go into the living room. Sitting down, Traci takes a good look at her friend. "So really, how are you holding up?"

"I'm not holding up, God is holding me. I feel like crawling into bed with the covers over me and never coming out. I'm hurt, I'm confused, but most of all I'm scared. Is he going to leave me for her? What will I do? What *do* I do?"

"Oh…I'm so sorry. I wish I could help you," Traci says.

Lost in her feelings, Sheila says, "I know that a lot of married couples break up and still live together, sleeping separately and living separate lives, but that's not us. Let me tell you, the other Sunday he made me dinner and we made love. So, we're not that couple, but in a way, we are. I don't know where we stand. I don't know what he's thinking. I want to tell him so badly that I know, but even more, I want him to tell me and try to make things work. So right now, I feel stuck." Sheila looks up at Traci with tears in her eyes. "At times, there are some nights I wake up looking to see if his home, especially if he's not in bed. I'm not going to lie…I go to the window to see if his car is there. You don't know what it feels like to be in love with a man who no longer loves you, or what it feels like to watch him get ready to go out somewhere without you. I gave that man all of me and I get this. I was a good wife. He was my best friend."

Traci reaches over and hugs Sheila as she cries. After she gets herself together, Sheila says, "Ok, that's enough of that. So, tell me, how are you doing?"

That's Traci's cue. "Well," she blurts out, "I like my stalker guy. We had a drink together and he has a 5-year-old daughter. So…now I told you."

"Oh, *wow*," Sheila says. "When and how did this happen?"

"I don't know, Sheila, it all just happened. I kept on running into him and he's new to the neighborhood. He asked me to show him around and he doesn't know anyone. And somehow, I couldn't stop thinking about him. And then a few days ago, I came out of the mall and he was there, honking his horn at me, and that's when we went out for a drink. And he told me about his situation with his ex-girlfriend and their daughter. I don't know why this is happening to me. I'm trying to stop it. But this man has invaded my inner thoughts."

Sheila says, "Well, you didn't do anything with this guy but talk and have drinks with him. That's all you did…right?"

"Yeah, that's all. Oh Sheila, I'm so sorry. I know what you're going through, but I had to get this off my chest."

"It's ok, don't worry about it," Sheila says.

"Ok…but this has never happened to me before. I never had any feelings for another man."

Paul wakes up thinking about Traci and their conversation, but he's mainly thinking about how he's starting to really feel her. *Who am I kidding?* he thinks. *I been had feelings for her ever since she worked at the club.* But now after seeing her again, the feelings have begun to resurface, and he wonders if she has any feelings for him. He's forgetting the fact that she's married, but remembers that she, too, has a 5-year-old, and that's something they have in common.

He lies in bed trying to think of a reason to call her, but the only thing that comes to mind is that he'll just call and thank her for seeing him the other day. He gets up the courage to call, not looking at the clock and realizing that it's 7:00 am on a Saturday morning. As the phone rings, he's not sure of what he'll say. As he listens to the third ring, going on its fourth, he starts to wonder if he's missed her until she finally answers.

"Hello?" Traci says, her voice still full of sleep.

"Hey, Traci. Did I catch you at a bad time?"

Traci rolls over in bed to see what time it is, and sees that it's 7:00 in the morning. She clears her throat. "No. Paul, is this you?"

"Yeah. I was just thinking about you and I wanted to thank you for your help and seeing me the other day."

"Oh, sure, no problem. Is everything ok? You're calling me so early in the morning…and you know I'm married?"

"Aww, Traci I'm so sorry. I just got so caught up in my thoughts that I didn't realize what time it is, nor was I thinking about you being married." He adds, "I'm sorry Traci. Yes, I've been having some issues regarding my daughter, but I've also been having some feelings for you. I know it's wrong for me to say this, but I like you a lot. I've liked you since when you were at the club, and now, seeing you again, all those feelings have come rushing back. We had good conversations, and I enjoyed being around you."

Traci is shocked, but she's also excited to hear that Paul has feelings for her. She lays there, smiling. *Oh no, this can't be happening. I'm married, and I love my family.* But when she responds she says, "Well, Paul, I'm flattered to hear this. And I have feelings for you too." She's surprised herself that she said it, and now she can't take it back.

Traci's husband, Steven, was up and out before 7:00 am to attend a men's day breakfast at church. Traci is glad that he's gone, for she would have had to explain this phone call. She's now so lost in her thoughts that she's forgotten she's still on the phone.

Paul is also lost in his thoughts, and now they both feel awkward and don't know what to say or do about their feelings or the situation. "Traci, I know this is sudden and awkward, but I feel relieved that you feel the same way," Paul finally says. "I'm just sorry about the situation."

SEVEN

Paul still has a few issues with Jasmine about this guy John being around Jacqueline. It's been a week since their last encounter, and he needs to get it off his chest. He calls her cell phone and leaves a message for her to call him ASAP.

Jasmine is surprised to see that Paul has called her, so she calls him back while on her break. Paul tells her again how he doesn't feel this guy should be around his daughter. "You're just jealous because I've found someone and you haven't," Jasmine says.

"No, Jazz, it's not that. I don't want no man around her to influence her or make her confused. I'm her father."

"Yes, I know that," Jasmine says, "and I told you I'm not trying to replace you as her father, you're a good father. Look, Paul, I have to go."

They hang up, but Paul isn't satisfied. He decides to take matters into his own hands and find out who this John guy is himself. He'll base it on what Jacqueline told him—that he drives a big truck, his workers talk funny and are tan color, and that John is brown.

The next day, Paul drives over to Jasmine's and parks not too far from her house early in the morning before she leaves for work. He doesn't have a clear view of the house from where he's parked, so he gets out and sees a truck pull up at the Fishers' house next door. Inside are two Mexicans and a black guy, who's on the phone while driving the truck. The Mexicans wait for him to open the front door. They all go inside, but a few minutes later he comes out and walks over to Jasmine's house, and Jasmine lets him in. Ten minutes later, they all come out. Jasmine straps Jacqueline into her car seat and closes the door, then stands there talking to John. Then, as they smile at each other, he hugs her and sneaks a kiss before waving goodbye to Jacqueline. He holds Jasmine's car door open for her to get in and shuts it. She pulls off, and he watches them drive away before turning back to the Fishers' house.

Paul quickly walks over. "Excuse me. I've seen you working on the Fisher house, and I want some work done to my place but I don't live in this neighborhood anymore. Do you do travel?"

"Yeah," says John. He walks to his truck and hands Paul a card.

"Ok. Good, because I live just two towns away."

"Oh, that's not too far. That's fine."

"Ok, good. Just let me gather a little more money together and I'll contact you." He looks at the card. "Oh, this is you? You John?"

"Yeah, this is my side business. I'm a professional licensed general contractor supervisor. Just call me when you're ready."

"Ok, thanks," Paul says. "That's good to know that you're a professional and not just a handyman." John walks toward the house. Paul looks at the card, then pulls out a pen and writes down John's license plate number. He walks away, feeling satisfied for the moment.

John and his men are almost finished at the Fishers' house. They should be done in two weeks. John feels a little sad because he'll miss his morning routine with Jasmine. He has some seriously strong feelings for her, but he's not sure where their relationship is going. *She sure got me to do some work on her house for almost nothing,* he thinks. *I charged her only for the labor because I had to pay my workers. And she bought a few things herself, but I ate a lot of the cost.*

The next morning, Paul gets up early and gets dressed to head back to Jasmine's, where he watches John and his workers arrive. This time, Paul can park in an excellent spot where he has full view of the house. Once again, John lets his workers into the Fishers' house before he goes next door to Jasmine's and she lets him in. They come out about 15 minutes later and Jacqueline is put into the car seat. John and Jasmine talk a little, and they hug and kiss before she leaves.

Paul continues to watch for another 20 minutes until John comes out of the Fishers' house and gets into his truck. Paul follows him as John drives over two townships. *He's going into my township,* Paul says to himself. John turns right on Pike Street, then makes a left onto Cherry Oak Drive. He turns into the driveway of a nice house, about three homes down on the left.

Paul stops at the corner, where he watches him get

out and take the trash cans off the curb and then finally go into the house. *This must be his house,* he thinks, and Paul wonders if he's ever brought Jasmine over there. He doesn't see another car in the driveway, but since it's still early decides to come back later.

He goes home and calls Jasmine. "What's wrong now, Paul?" she says as she answers.

"I just want to know how well you know this guy."

"Paul, please stop this. He's a nice guy and I really like him."

"Well, have you been to his place?"

"I just told you to stop it."

"Well, have you? I take that as a no."

"Ok, no, and that don't mean nothing." She adds, "You need to go back to work now, because you clearly need something to do. I don't know how your job let you take a month off." Paul loves his job as an investment advisor for a large, well-known financial investment firm in Philadelphia, and he's good at what he does.

"I told you, I can't carry over any more hours. I've reached the maximum so I must take off. I'm not giving them all these hours."

"Ok, well, leave it alone, Paul. I'm hanging up before you get me fired."

After hanging up with Jasmine, Paul suspects something's not right with this John guy. He wants to see for himself what he's about, so he decides to go back to his house. He gets there just in time to see a car pull up in the driveway and park right next to John's truck. A woman gets out and uses a key to enter to the house. *What? This guy is married?* He wonders. Now he questions whether Jasmine knows that her little so-called boyfriend is married.

Paul is angry. He had followed John home because he wanted to confront him and tell him to stay away from his daughter, but when John gets to his house Paul decides that Jasmine is the one he should be confronting, so he goes to her house instead. He rings the doorbell.

"Paul," Jasmine says, surprised to see him as she opens the door. "What's wrong? Why you are here?"

Paul walks in without waiting for her to close the door. "Where's Jacqueline?"

"She's at my mom's."

"Oh, that's what you do when you have your man over? You send your daughter to your mom's?"

"What are you talking about?"

"What, are you telling me I'm wrong?" Paul says.

Jasmine doesn't want to hear his mouth, so she says no. "Wow. Now you're starting to lie to me," Paul says. "I rode by here twice a few nights ago and I saw his truck. And I was here that morning also when he left and saw you waving him bye at the door with your robe on. Yeah, I saw you, and I saw him here before too. And you want to know what? I followed him to his home and I came back later and guess what I saw, his wife. So now you like seeing married men. So, I guess that's why he hasn't invited you to his nice house, because his wife is there. So that's why he can only come to see you and you take our daughter to your mom's." Paul is furious. "Do I have it right?"

"Yeah Paul, that's right. Oh, you're stalking me again. Hmm. You and I are so over, Paul, so you need to move on."

"No, once again, this is not about you, it's about

our daughter."

"Yeah, I bet. And I keep telling you to call me, don't just stop by."

"Oh, what, because of your boyfriend? I'm going to always ride by and check up on you, even though we're not together. We have a long history together and you're the mother of my child."

"Paul, look," Jasmine says, "thanks for watching over us. I do appreciate it. But who I see is no longer your concern."

"But that's where you're wrong, because what affects our daughter also affects me. Look, all I've been trying to say is just be careful and selective as to who you allow to be around Jacqueline. She's young and she's watching and learning things from you. So, the things you are showing her now will have a lasting effect on her future regarding men and life in general."

Jasmine can't get mad, because what he's saying is the truth. That's why she's trying to step up things with John, because she feels he's the one for her and she's trying to be the one for him. *Things are going well so far, especially after last night,* she thinks. *I can't have Paul messing things up for me.*

EIGHT

One day at work, Sheila's boss, Mr. Gilford, comes into Sheila's office. "My case load is full, and I have a case where this woman wants her husband investigated. She believes he's cheating. And I believe you're ready for this type of case. If you need my advice, just let me know. I know things are tight and you've been doing the receptionist work as well as your own," he adds. "I know we need to hire a new receptionist, so if you know someone let me know."

"Thank you for the case! And yes, if I think of someone I'll let you know." Then she says, "I'll follow you to your office to get the client's information and I'll contact her tomorrow for a consultation." She gets the file from Mr. Gilford, leaves his office, and returns to her own. *Oh God, I can't do this,* she thinks. *This is too close to my own situation. But maybe that's the reason why I should do this…I can help women who've been put into this situation.* She thinks about who she knows that can fill the receptionist position and then remembers Jasmine, the receptionist at her dentist's office. She grabs her pocketbook to look for her number, then calls her.

Jasmine answers the phone to an unknown caller, something she doesn't normally do. But she picks it up and answers it. "Hi, Jasmine, this is Sheila. You know me from the dentist's office. You told me a few months ago that you need a job and well, I'm calling you because my office—I work at an investigating agency—we need a receptionist. My boss just asked me if I know of someone and I thought of you, so I'm calling you to see if you're interested."

"Yes! I'm interested," Jasmine says.

"Ok, good! I'll tell my boss and I'll be in touch." Now that that's solved, Sheila takes the folder of her new case and looks at the little bit of information that's in there. She decides to call the client now instead of tomorrow, so she dials Mrs. Tiffany Turner.

Mrs. Turner answers the phone. It's about 2:45 pm on a Monday afternoon. Sheila introduces herself and states that she will be handling her case and that she would like to meet with her for a consultation. "I can come in Wednesday at 10:00 am if that's ok with you," Mrs. Turner says.

"That's fine. I'll see you on Wednesday."

Sheila goes home, emotionally exhausted and it's only the first day of a new week. Her weekend was quiet and she didn't go anywhere, not even to church on Sunday. It's not, however, about what she *didn't* do, but about what she *did*. She pulled out her wedding album and started looking at the pictures, and if that wasn't enough, she watched the wedding video to top things off. She cried for over two hours. wondering what happened and if there was anything she could have done to have prevented this from happening. She wondered why he didn't tell her they were in trouble or what he needed more from her. She cried over the fact that he never gave her a chance, and wondered when he stopped loving her. She had thought they were a happy married couple, and she wanted to have his child. *Yes, we had some problems, but I didn't think it would result in him desiring another woman and cheating on me,* she thought. *I didn't deserve to be disrespected.* She cried herself to sleep.

Tonight, Sheila's drained and emotionally spent. She fixes something to eat, something light and quick before going to bed.

Wednesday is the day Sheila meets her new client, Mrs. Turner, and she's extremely nervous. Her case hits close to home and makes it that much more real for her. She thinks that this is her trial run before she investigates her own husband, John.

She walks out of her office and goes to the receptionist desk to Jasmine, whose first day is today. She asks her to set up the conference room with coffee, water, and tea, and a tray with about five assorted pastries for her meeting. She goes back into her office and says a quick prayer to calm herself down while she waits for her client to arrive. Ten minutes later, Jasmine calls her to announce that Mrs. Turner is here.

Sheila comes out of her office to greet Mrs. Turner, extending her hand and introducing herself. Like she did with Ms. Amanda, she sizes her up and thinks about what an attractive woman she is. Mrs. Turner has a pretty face, with a nice shape, up-to-date haircut, and nice taste in clothes and shoes. She is very fashionable. After they shake hands, Sheila leads her into the conference room and offers her some of what Jasmine has placed on the table for them.

"Thank you, I'll take a cup of coffee and a danish," Mrs. Turner says.

"Sure, help yourself." Sheila adds, "Before we get started, I want to make sure the financial part was made clear to you. The retainer cost for my services is $1000 plus expenses. I will send you emails regarding the fees on an Excel expense form so you can see where your money is going. Do you have any questions?"

"No," Mrs. Turner answers.

"One more thing. Are you able to pay the retainer charge today?"

"Yes, and I'm prepared to also pay $500 toward the miscellaneous fees."

"Ok. Before you leave you can pay the receptionist. Ok, so tell me why you're here and what you expect from me," Sheila says. "But first tell me a little history about yourself and your marriage."

Mrs. Tiffany Turner begins, "My husband's name is Richard, and we've been married for 18 years. We have three kids, one boy and two girls. Our oldest is 19 and she has two more years of college to go." Turning serious, she says, "Well, it started about five years ago. I noticed little changes in his actions and his attitude slowly started to change. Overall, our marriage is like an average one—we have our ups and downs. Some were serious, but we managed to get through them over time. But these past two years have been very difficult and hard on me." Her eyes turn sad. "Richard is a good man. He's a hard worker, but I really believe his change has something to do with a woman. You see, we're both pretty much outgoing people, and we do things both separately and together. Well, at least we did up until about three months before our youngest went to college. Richard started spending more time without me. There have been times he told me he was with one of our friends and he wasn't. I called the friend's house and they told me no, they weren't together, then I pretended by saying, 'Oh, I thought he said y'all went out.' And then I asked for his wife even though I really didn't want to talk to her. And that made me feel like he's keeping secrets. What is he hiding? The not knowing is what's getting to me. I've been trying to talk to him about anything when he is home. I'm doing that so maybe he'll say something that may give me some clues as to what's going on with him. But even that's not working, because for the most part his answers are short and this whole thing is driving me crazy. There have been times when I suggested that we go out and he just says no, he's tired. And to be more personal, he's even refused my sexual advances, and that's something he rarely did."

"Yes, I understand," Sheila says. What she really wants to say is, *Girl, I'm so feeling you. And trust me, if that dog is cheating on you I will catch him, believe me.* Instead she says, "Did you bring me a recent picture of him?" She hands her a piece of paper and pen. "And can you list some of the places you know where he goes?"

Tiffany takes the paper and writes down all the places that she's aware of where Richard goes, then hands it back to Sheila along with a photo of Richard. Sheila looks at the picture. *WOW, this man is fine,* she thinks to herself. She asks Tiffany to verify their address for her, because in the next few days she'll be starting her surveillance. She then asks her what time he leaves out for work.

"He normally leaves the house around 7:00 or 7:15 am."

"Ok. Well, do you have any questions for me?"

"Yes, about how long will it take?"

"It could take a month or it could take five months, it all depends on Richards's actions. But I will be giving you updates."

"Ok, I guess I'll just have to wait it out now. Thank you."

"I'll be in touch with you as soon as I get something," Sheila says, getting up from her chair. "I have everything I need for now. You can pay Jasmine, the receptionist." Tiffany gets up too. She thanks her again, and they shake hands before she walks out the room and heads for the receptionist desk.

Sheila goes back to her office, even more eager to find out what this guy Richard's story is. She looks at this very attractive, mid to late 40-something-year-old man. The picture appears to show him with a muscular build, with a cropped salt and pepper haircut.

She arrives at the Turners' home on Friday, day one of her surveillance, camera in hand and ready to take pictures of Richard and follow his whereabouts. She parks where she has a full view of the house. Twenty minutes later, the front door opens and out walks Richard, who is *fine* with his brown-skinned self. He gets into his Lincoln, which looks well taken care of. They live in a nice neighborhood—not the best, but it's far from the worst. Richard also looks like a nice dresser.

Sheila follows Richard, who seems to be heading

to work. He drives about 30 minutes from home and pulls into the parking lot of a business complex. She stops just short of the parking lot entrance, just enough so she can see him get out of his car and go into the building as she snaps pictures of him.

She leaves and returns at 3:30 pm, an hour before he gets off work, according to the information Tiffany has given her. This time, she parks in the lot as close as she can and still have a good view of him. While she sits and waits, she looks at her emails and does a little reading from one of her favorite author's books. Before she knows it, she hears people and a few car engines, and she realizes it's 4:25 pm. She puts her book down and starts to watch for Richard, who finally comes out around 4:40. He gets into his car and Sheila pulls out slowly after him, following close enough but not enough that he would notice her. He stops into a small café, and Sheila snaps a few pictures of him going inside. A few minutes later, she takes some more pictures when she sees him sitting, alone, by the window. He sits for about an hour, eating and drinking something. He leaves the café, then sits in his car on the phone for another half hour before he starts the car and pulls off. Was he talking to the person he was supposed to be meeting up with? He pulls off, driving slowly, almost as if he's trying to kill time, before finally ending up home by 6:20 pm.

Days four and five are the same, but by day ten, a Saturday, things are a little different. Richard is up and out the house by 8:45 am, and Sheila is right there behind him. His first stop is the barber shop. It looks like he's going to be there for a while, so she settles in with her phone and charger. She checks her emails, sends texts, and browses through Facebook. She also has her book to read, and has brought food and two bottles of water, one frozen. But there's one thing she's forgotten about: nature calls. Her bladder is too full and she has to relieve herself, so now she has to leave to find a fairly clean restroom, because Sheila has a thing about using public restrooms.

She looks in on Richard, who seems to have three heads before him. She leaves on her quest to finding a decent restroom, and in ten minutes she finds one in a nearby Target. It's still early so it's been barely used, and Sheila is happy for that. She rushes back to the barber shop and she is lucky to get her same parking spot. By now, Richard is the barber's chair.

After he leaves, he drives to that same café. Instead of going inside the café, he heads towards a black Cadillac parked nearby and gets in on the passenger side. He sits in the car for an hour before he and an anonymous person step out of the vehicle. Sheila's ready with camera in hand to snap some pictures, and as the door opens she anticipates a beautiful young woman stepping out. As Sheila watches through her camera lens, she first sees a pair of legs, then looks up to see a nicely shaped, very attractive older woman, and her mouth drops open. This woman appears to be at least in her mid-60s. At first Sheila thinks it may be his mom or older sister—until she watches them kiss. She almost forgets she's working a case, because she pictures John kissing her like that. She quickly snaps some shots of them kissing before they go into the café.

The next time, she captures pictures of them entering a hotel about a mile or two away from home, where they stay for most of the day.

Sheila follows them two more times before she

reports to set up a meeting. She's been so busy that she hasn't had a chance to talk to Jasmine. Today, however, she has some extra time, and she asks her how she's making out and if she has any questions about anything.

Jasmine says she has no questions, and Sheila asks how she likes working here. They catch up on some girl talk, then Sheila asks her about Paul. "Oh girl, me and Paul been broke up. In fact, he moved I think to the next town or two over. But anyway, I got a new man and I plan on keeping him."

"Well, that's good as long as he treats you good. Where'd you meet him at?"

"I didn't have to go far. I was pulling out of my driveway and he nearly hit me. He was doing some work on my neighbor's house, and you know I had some words for him." The phone rings, so Jasmine answers it.

Sheila meets with Mrs. Turner, and she gives her the photos of her husband with the older woman. Mrs. Turner is nervous as she takes the envelope and slowly pulls out the photos. Her tears begin to fall silently before she looks up. "She's older. He's cheating on me with an older woman. I don't know how I should feel about it. I just knew she was younger and she's just playing games with him. But this is a woman, not a chick, and a seasoned woman at that." She looks at Sheila. "How do I handle this? What does that mean? She looks to be at least 17 years older. I have so many questions. What could they want with each other? How long have they been seeing each other? Where did they first meet? Is she a co-worker?" Mrs. Turner looks to Sheila for these answers, though she knows she can't answer them.

Mrs. Turner's attitude changes from hurt to anger, and Sheila asks her what she plans on doing. "Oh no, he's not getting away with this. I'm going to confront him and get some answers, you better believe that. I gave him the best of me. Yeah, we had our moments but we bounced back—or at least I thought."

Her words strike a chord with Sheila, because she too thought she and her own husband had also bounced back from their problems. Just then, something changes within her and she knows what she must do: she's going to investigate him. She already knows where he lives and she thinks she, too, will get to the bottom of this. She had forgotten where she was for a moment until she hears Mrs. Turner calling her name and asking if is she okay.

"What? What, oh, yes I'm sorry. I'm fine. I just got lost in my own thoughts."

"Oh. So what do I do now?"

"I can continue the investigation and follow him some more, or we can just end it here. It's up to you."

"You have confirmed my suspicions. I guess that's all." They conclude their business, and Mrs. Turner pays Jasmine and leaves.

Sheila goes back into her office to close out Mrs. Turner's case, her mind racing all the while about following John. She emails Mr. Gilford to request four days off, and states that she just closed her last open case. Even though in a few weeks she'll be on a one-week vacation, she's entitled to two weeks. She doesn't know when she'll use her last week yet.

Later within that hour, Mr. Gilford calls her into his office. Once inside, Sheila closes the door and takes a seat. He asks her if everything is all right, then says, "You're scheduled for a vacation in a few weeks, am I correct?"

"Yes, but it's for a personal matter," is all she says. Sheila is a private person and rarely talks about her personal life.

Mr. Gilford looks at her and says, "Okay, I'll give you the four days."

Sheila gets up, thanks him, and returns to her office to continue preparing additional notes for Jasmine to type up for their quarterly reports.

NINE

After her meeting with Sheila, Lady Campbell has begun to feel her burden and goes into prayer on her behalf. She's been where Sheila's at, and she knows all too well how dark of a place it can be. She wanted to show Sheila that she can relate to her pain, and so she freely became an open book in exposing herself to Sheila. She hopes that by sharing her experience, which was like Sheila's (except that she had been engaged, not married), has helped detour Sheila from pursuing things herself. But talking about her experience has made Lady Campbell realize just how far she herself has come, and how if it wasn't for the grace and mercy of God carrying her that she doesn't know where she'd be today.

Sheila appeared to be frazzled and she also seemed quite angry and bitter, which caused Lady Campbell to become alarmed. When Sheila broke down and cried, Lady Campbell could connect to her emotions then. She related to Sheila's feelings of being broken, hurt, and betrayed. Lady Campbell knows about the waves of emotions, and how you want to pretend nothing has happened as you begin to mask your emotions and try to elude the fact that your world has been affected. But in reality, you're devastated and your world has actually crashed into millions of pieces. She can imagine how Sheila feels that her marriage has all been a lie and that her dreams for their future are all gone. You wonder how long has this been happening and how many others there have been. And, of course, she's wondering who else knows. So as she attempts to deal with her embarrassment, Lady Campbell sees exactly where Sheila's at. She knows that, at this stage, she's very fragile and could go either way. One more devastating thing can take her over the edge.

Traci calls Sheila. This time, she comes right out and says, "Hey, girl, I need to see you. Can I come over?"

"Yeah, I could use some company. John went out again and I'm feeling some type of way," Sheila answers.

"Ok, I'll be there soon."

Within half an hour, Traci is ringing Sheila's doorbell. Sheila opens the door. Her eyes are puffy and red, as if she's been crying. Traci walks in. She goes right into the living room to her favorite chair and Sheila goes to the couch. "So what's going on with you? You said you needed to talk," Sheila says.

"Paul called me the other day."

"Ok...so who's Paul?"

"You know, the stalker guy."

"Oh. How did he get your number and what did he want?"

"I told you before that I ran into him and we went and had a drink and we talked. But I didn't tell you we exchanged numbers so I could show him around. He called just to thank me again for the other night, and then he told me that he has feelings for me. And for some reason, I told him that I have feelings for him too. I don't know why I said it, it just came out. And now I don't know what to do."

"Wow, what made you tell him that?"

"I don't know. I was listening to him and feeling everything he was saying and before I knew it I was telling him that I was feeling him too. The words just came out and I couldn't stop it. The funny thing is, he said he felt relieved and so do I. Oh Sheila, I can't stop myself from thinking about him. This is crazy. I love my husband, so why in the world am I having these feelings for Paul?"

Sheila sits there, thinking, *What is this? This must be a joke. Here I'm wanting my husband and he's cheating on me, and she's sitting up here talking about her feelings for this man who's not her husband.* "I think we both need to talk to Lady Campbell."

"Ok, maybe you're right. I guess it couldn't hurt anything."

Sheila gets her cell phone and calls Lady Campbell. When she answers, Sheila tells her what's going on with herself as well as with Traci. Lady Campbell tells them to meet her at the church. Sheila hangs up and tells Traci.

Lady Campbell gets to the church and turns on some lights, then goes into her office. She sits at her desk and she begins to pray to get her mind settled before they arrive.

Traci and Sheila drive their own cars so Traci can

go home from there. They get to the church and ring the doorbell, since they're the only ones there. Lady Campbell comes to the door and greets them with a hug. Traci looks scared. "Don't worry, everything will be fine," Lady Campbell says, patting her hand.

Lady Campbell leads them into her office. Traci and Sheila sit on the couch and Lady Campbell sits in a chair. Lady Campbell says, "Well, before we start let's say a word of prayer." She prays for peace of mind, clarity and wisdom, then says, "Sheila tells me that the both of you are having some issues that need some attention."

"Yes," Sheila answers. "I can't take no more of this. I had to watch him tonight get ready to go out. And for the life of me, I don't know why, but each time he leaves I go to the window and I watch him pull off. I just want him to have that change of heart and come back in and stay with me. But that doesn't happen and each time he pulls away I cry. And tonight, before he went out, he tried to make small talk about what I was looking at on my laptop, trying to act as if he was interested and have a little conversation with me when he peeked at my laptop and saw the article of Jay-Z and Beyoncé's sister. I was choking on my words because I was on the verge of telling him everything. It felt like he was playing games with me. So now I'm beyond being hurt…I'm also angry. And I need to get this out in the open. I'm telling him tonight."

Concerned, Lady Campbell looks at Sheila. "Are you sure you really want to do this?"

Sheila returns her gaze. "No, but I have to do it anyway. I can't keep on watching him leave me."

"Ok, but brace yourself for his anger and his lies,

because you know he's going to deny it."

"But I still have to let him know anyway. I can no longer let him get away with this."

"You know I'm here for you," Lady Campbell says. "Now it's your turn, Traci."

Traci says, "There's a guy from my past who I used to do private dances for. We mostly talked. We had real good conversations, and I kind of liked him. Well, to make a long story short, he saw me and I thought he was a stalker until he ran into me at the market. He explained how he's new to the area and that he's been seeing me around but wasn't sure until that moment, and that's when I recognized him. We talked for a few minutes, and the next time we ran into each other he asked me if I could show him around. I told him I'm married and I have a 5-year-old son. He said, 'Oh, well if you don't mind,' and I told him we'd work something out. Then there was another time when I came out of the mall and he was there, and told me he was looking for me and could we go somewhere to talk and have a drink. He followed me to the restaurant two towns over. He was upset because his daughter's mother has been allowing the guy she's dating to come to the house and be around his daughter."

"Ok," Lady Campbell says, "When y'all went to the restaurant why did you go two towns over? And when did you realize your feelings were coming back for him?"

Traci says, "I didn't want anyone seeing me with him and assuming things. And yet after talking with him I discovered that he has a 5-year-old like me. The more we talked it felt familiar, and since that day he has invaded my thoughts. I don't understand why this is happening. I love Steven, my husband."

"You know, sometimes we look to other people outside of ourselves for things we're lacking within us," Lady Campbell says. "And that means in your marriage, your boyfriend, your family dynamics, any type of relationship you have. If there's a need and you're lacking something, what comes natural to us is to seek it elsewhere. But what's natural is not always the right thing to do."

"I guess you're right," Traci says as she thinks, *Things have changed with Steven and me. He used to have more time to spend with me and now it's more like he's too busy with work and church. I feel like he's forgotten about me. And don't let me get started with all the things I do, as well. So yes, you are right. I feel neglected. Wow, and I guess because I had previously liked Paul it was so easy and natural for me to fall back into that place where I once was.*

Traci smiles. "Thank you for helping me realize this. Now the question still is, what do I do with these feelings? How do I turn them off? And how do I get back in the right place with my husband? Can this be fixed?"

"Oh yes," says Lady Campbell, "there is nothing too hard for God. Don't underestimate the power of the Lord." She looks at Sheila. "That applies to you too. Well, I think we accomplished a lot tonight and we need to meet in, let's say, three weeks. But if you need to meet sooner just let me know." They all leave out together to go home.

When Sheila came home from meeting with Lady Campbell, she was ready to confront John. She'd had her words ready but he was not home yet, so she waited in the living room watching TV and finally fell asleep. When she woke up by 12:15 am, she realized he wasn't coming home so she turned off the TV and went upstairs to bed. At first she was a little concerned, but then she figured that he must have stayed the night with her. She got into bed, her heart breaking once more. Her mind unsettled, she tossed and turned before finally falling back to sleep.

She wakes up at 8:45, and remembers that John didn't come home. She gets up and goes to the window to see if his car is outside, but it isn't. She gets back into bed, at first starting to retreat but then thinking, *No, I want to be up and waiting to confront him in the living room when he comes in.* She gets up, makes the bed and takes her shower, then throws on sweatpants and a shirt before going downstairs to wait for John. She prays for the strength and courage to confront him and get this out in the open.

John drives home, not thinking about Jasmine but about what's he's going to say to Sheila. It's 10:15 when he gets home, and he pulls up in front of the house and sits in the car for a minute as he tries to get himself together. He gets out, hits the alarm, walks up the steps, puts the key in and opens the door. He walks in to see Sheila sitting in the living room, not looking happy at all. "Oh, you scared me," he says nervously.

"Yeah. What were you doing last night that you come home now at 10:18 and as soon as you see me you're scared? Tell me, John, where were you?"

John starts fumbling with his words until Sheila interrupts him. "Don't you dare lie to me, John."

He takes a breath, blows it out, and sits on the couch because Sheila is sitting in the chair across from the coffee table. He needs something between them when he tells her the truth. He begins with, "I love you."

Sheila stops him. "John, you have the nerve to say you love me when you've spent the night out cheating on me?" He looks shocked. "Yes, I know, John. I've known for a few months and it's been the hardest thing I've had to deal with. Four months ago I called you because you neglected to call and tell me that you were coming home late. You told me you were at Lowe's pricing out some things for a potential job. We hung up and your phone redialed me, but I didn't answer and it went to my voice mail. Your phone had pocket dialed me, John, and I heard a female say, 'John, you don't know what you want.' And then my world stopped when I heard you clearly tell this woman, 'I know what I want, and I want you.' Do you know how devastating it is to unexpectedly hear the husband that you love tell another woman that he wants her?" Sheila looks at him as her tears flow openly. She begins to sob as she reveals the pain which she can no longer hide.

"I'm so sorry for causing you pain," John says. "I do love you but I'm not in love with you. And yes, I've been cheating on you. I met her while doing a side job. And no, she didn't hire me to do a job; she's a neighbor to a job I was doing. It just happened, I don't know what to tell you. I wasn't planning for this to happen. Please believe me, Sheila. I see how much I've hurt you. What do you want me to do? This has been hard on me and I'm very confused."

"Do you love her?" Sheila asks.

"No, and that's the truth."

"You need to move out so I can figure things out

and you can do whatever you want to do."

"Ok, but can I stay until I find a place?"

"Ok, but you'll be sleeping in the guest room, starting tonight." Sheila gets up and goes to her room. She cries as her marriage and her life crumples before her eyes. She always wanted him to confess and now that he has after confronting him, things has changed and she's even more hurt. She sits on the bed, wondering what she'll do now.

John remains seated on the couch, his head leaned back against the cushions and his eyes closed as he rubs his temples. His head is really hurting. The stress and pressure of everything has likely caused his blood pressure to rise. John wonders if it has all been worth it, and now he is the cause of their breakup.

Over the next long week, they walk around each other, Sheila not speaking because of her pain and John not speaking because he doesn't know what to say that will change things. By Friday night, John has just about finished packing. He's been coming home every night and getting on the computer to look for an apartment. He found one by Wednesday, and after work on Thursday saw the place, paid for it, and received his keys. So now, this is his last night home with his wife, and he has so many mixed feelings going on inside of him.

One is that he doesn't want to leave, because even though he's not in love with her he still loves her. The other part is that he knows that he never really gave her a chance to make things right. Now he's at this place that he brought her to, all because of his selfishness. Now they both hurt, but her pain is unexpected and much deeper.

Once John finishes packing, he looks for Sheila.

He knocks on her bedroom door, which she keeps closed now. "Come in."

John opens the door and comes in. "Well, I'm finished packing and I've found a place, so in the morning I'll be going." He looks her in the eyes. "Sheila, I'm really sorry. If you need me, please call me."

As soon as John leaves, Sheila immediately notices the silence and it makes her feel alone. She couldn't say anything to him when he told her that everything was packed and he was leaving, because she was an emotional wreck and knew if she said anything, she'd end up asking him to stay and she knew he needed to go.

The first few weeks are just awful. Sheila cries a lot, and hates coming home to an empty house. She almost calls him just to talk, thinking that if she hears his voice maybe she can calm down and be ok. But she decides against calling him because she doesn't want to make him think that she's desperate. So she focuses her energy on cleaning the house, a little bit every night. She does a thorough cleaning, something that's long overdue, and helps her to keep her mind off of things. And of course, she has Traci and Lady Campbell to talk to during the rough nights.

In one week, it'll be a month since John has left. Even though it still hurts, Sheila is finding the courage and strength to survive. She gets up every morning and thanks God for allowing her to see another day, a new day with another chance to get it right. She gets up even when she doesn't want to, but she has to pay the bills now. She thinks about how John would never tell her how much the bills were whenever she asked, but would just say he'd show her when he finds wherever he put them at and would get mad if she asked again. So, Sheila is a little surprised at how much the bills actually are when they come, but somehow she's able to pay them all, though it leaves her with hardly anything left over. But all her bills are paid and she has food in the house. It's tight, but she's done it and proud that she was able to do it. She thanks God for her job and the raise they gave her after proving herself when they gave her a case. They had told her there would also be bonuses as well as a yearly raise.

But she's now a broken woman, whose emotions are on ten because her hurt has become more like resentful anger. The quietness has really got her thinking, and she feels somewhat like a fool. As she reflects on many past situations she now sees John as controlling. And that he took full advantage of her, knowing that she would do anything just to keep the peace between them. But each time she brought her issues to him as the head of their household. So, they could discuss and resolve them, he would turn it into an argument and leave the house. She realizes now that she allowed hers needs and desires to be neglected because she didn't love herself enough to do like he did and put herself first and stand her ground. But now it's time that she gets reacquainted with herself.

John moves into his apartment with mixed feelings. He understands that Sheila's hurt, but he feels she's going a little too far with kicking him out of his house. He should have told her that he wasn't leaving his house, that he'd put too much into it. But for once he admits that he'd thought about her feelings, not his, and instead just gave in.

His apartment is a large, one-bedroom with up-to-date appliances, a large walk-in closet, a balcony and a laundry room on each floor of the building. John likes it, but it's not home. He meets a few of his neighbors, who all seem nice. When he left, he'd told Sheila he was taking the basement furniture with him, and she agreed. The furniture he took made for a complete living room set, though he had to buy a bedroom and small dinette set, as well as some other things to complete his place. It would take some getting used to.

It's one week shy of being a month of living on his own, and he's had time to think about what's really happening to him. But he truly doesn't know how it all just happened; it just did.

Jasmine calls him, though he hasn't talked to her in a few weeks. He tells her it's nothing personal against her but that he just needs some time to himself. He says that a lot has been happening and he needs some time to process things. She offers to help him but he says no, he'd call her in a few days, and they hang up.

Over the next couple of days, John just works and goes home. He wants to call Sheila to see if she's ok and if she needs anything, but he doesn't want to look desperate. So one night when he knows she'll be home, or at least when she would normally be home, he drives slowly by the house to check up on her. He sees her car in the driveway, which makes him feel happy knowing she's home and safe, and goes back to his apartment.

It's the beginning of the month, time to pay the bills. This time, John's bills are less than usual, making him happy on one end and yet worried on the other. He wonders if Sheila will be able to maintain the upkeep of the house and the household bills. He doesn't want to lose the house, mainly because he invested too much into it but also because most of the bills are in his name and he doesn't want his credit being affected. So he decides to call her to see if she needs a little help with the bills, since he's the cause of the whole situation in the first place. As he calls, he wonders why he's nervous as he listens to the phone ring.

"Hello?" Sheila finally answers after the third ring.

Pausing for half a second, he says, "Hi, hey, how are you doing?"

"I'm ok."

"I was just checking to see if you need anything or if you want me to do something."

"Something like what?"

"I don't know. Fix something or help you pay a bill or two."

"Oh no, I've managed to pay the bills this month. But I will keep your offer in mind for the following months. Thanks for offering, John…I appreciate it." What she also wants to say is, *What you should be offering is to pay the two highest bills, or at least the mortgage.*

John feels her attitude shifting, so he just says, "Ok. Just let me know when I can help you with anything."

"Ok, John. I've got to go." She hangs up.

John looks at the phone. She'd hung up before he had chance to say goodbye, goodnight, good riddance. He hangs up, feeling uneasy. He wonders what's wrong with her but finally just brushes it off.

Sheila wakes up extremely nervous as she prepares to stake out John. Her thoughts are all over the place. But she convinces herself that she just wants to see the woman that has stolen her husband form her. But the reality is that in her brokenness she is also insecure. And she wants to catch them together to see how he acts with her so she can compare how he was with herself.

Sheila has always been a sweet, quiet woman who doesn't draw attention to herself, so she stays behind the shadows. But John has changed this untainted woman into a woman scorned. Sheila has taken this way beyond herself, for its more than personal—it's her business.

She leaves the house and travels to John's apartment, then waits for him to come out. He comes out and drives right to work, which today is a construction site. His company has a two-year contract to build a new senior citizen community complex in an up and coming area of the city.

Sheila settles in for the wait. John leaves the work site twice and each time she follows him, nervously anticipating him going to see some woman, but each time he doesn't. Once he goes to the office and the other time he gets some lunch. Sheila leaves to go to the restroom twice in her almost eight-hour surveillance of her husband.

Sheila goes home, emotionally exhausted and a little stiff. But she's glad she didn't catch John with this female, because she swears she doesn't know what she would have done. As day one comes to an end, she goes into the bathroom and takes a long, hot shower.

By Saturday, day six, she plans to follow him all

day, because she feels sooner or later he's going to see this other woman today. He goes out a couple times and then comes back home, staying inside for hours. Sheila wonders if he's sleeping.

But John is in the house relaxing, while trying to get up enough nerve to call Sheila. He's given his feelings about their situation a great deal of thought, though he still has no real answer or clarity as to how he allowed this whole thing to happen. "Here we go," he says to himself, and calls Sheila.

Sheila is still parked outside of his apartment when, surprisingly, her phone rings, and she instantly panics as she looks at the phone's display and realizes it's John. *Does he know I've been following him? Did he see me?* she thinks. She answers the phone with a slightly disturbed attitude to throw him off.

"Yeah? I mean hello?"

Her tone must have worked because he says, "Ah, hey Sheila. It's John, how you doing? Did I catch you at a bad time?"

Sheila realizes that he doesn't know anything, so she quickly changes her attitude from bothered to a little more accepting. "I'm doing ok, how about you?"

"I'm doing ok too. I'm calling because we haven't talked in a while and I want to keep our communication lines open." John calls her for two reasons: one, he wants to know how is she making out maintaining the house and paying the bills, although he would never dare mention that to her. And the other reason is because he still loves her and he's kind of missing her being around.

"Oh you do, do you?"

"Come on Sheila, don't be like that. I've been racking my brain on how and why this all happened, and I cannot come up with a definite answer. You know we've had our many challenges, and you've been really pressuring me about having a child and just nagging me about little stuff. I realize your internal clock is ticking, but I just wanted us to be financially stable first before we add any additions to our family."

"Ok, I do understand that, but I can't understand you cheating on me. If we were in trouble you should have told me."

"That's just it, Sheila, we weren't in trouble. That's the thing, that's why I can't explain what happened."

"Even so, it wouldn't have happened if you hadn't allowed it, John, so I don't want to hear it."

"Come on Sheila, give me a break."

"Isn't that something? Give *you* a break? John, you're full of it. I didn't get no break, did I? I didn't get nothing, not even a warning. And the fact that you walked around here pretending that everything is good when you been cheating, that hurts, and especially to find out the way I did. And you have the nerve to say give you a break? You got to be kidding me."

"Ok, ok, Sheila you're right. Just calm down. I know I deserve that and you didn't deserve what I did. I just want to know what do we do now, where do we go from here?"

"Do you love her?"

John sighs. "Honestly, I have some strong feelings for her."

"Well then, do you know how you feel about me?"

John says, "Sheila, I still love you but I'm not quite sure if I'm in love with you."

"So, are you telling me she has a piece of your

heart? And what, now you're confused about whether you're in love with me or not. Wow, John, I see she's gotten into your head. Wow, I don't know where we go from here. Look, this is too much…I got to go." Sheila hangs up, hurt and angry. All she wants to do is go home, but she waits a half an hour before leaving just in case he goes out. He doesn't so she calls it a night, feeling hot, angry tears welling up in her eyes.

Sheila made the appointment with her pastor two weeks ago for John and herself, and now the time has arrived. Pastor and Lady Campbell greet them, and then they pray and get right into it.

They ask who would like to start, and John says for Sheila to go ahead. "Should I start from the beginning?" Sheila asks. Lady Campbell says yes.

"I discovered John was cheating on me by a recorded voicemail. That day my very foundation was shattered and I was devastated. Yes, we had our share of problems but we seemed to always overcome them. I never saw this coming. And I kept this for months hoping he would have a change of heart and tell me himself, and that we can try to fix what's not working. But that never happened. And it was hurting too much. I finally confronted him and he admitted it, and now he lives in an apartment."

Lady Campbell says, "Ok John, tell us what's going on."

John clears his throat. "Well, what she said is all true. But, I wasn't looking for anyone. You see, I wasn't overly happy but I also wasn't miserably unhappy either. It honestly was something that just happened."

"Nothing just happens," Pastor says. "You have to

want it or you just allowed it."

"Well, I guess I don't know, a little of both. I was going to a job site and as I pulled up to the location our vehicles almost collided. She jumped out and cursed me out. I apologized and she did too. I introduced myself, and the next day I kind of made sure I saw her to speak to her, and then the next thing I know I started to like her."

"Ok," Pastor says, "but now I want you to tell me what happened between you and Sheila."

"I might have become numb to her and neglected her because of all of her nagging and her obsession with having a baby. So, I guess I detached myself from her and focused on work. I was avoiding her issues she had with me, because I was afraid I would not be a good father. I never had one. I would tell Sheila that we were not financially ready and that was partly true." John puts his head down.

"That's good, now we're getting to the truth," Pastor says. "Her pressure and your fears of being a father pushed you away from her. And then you meet this other woman who you know nothing about and you find yourself attracted to her, but what really attracts you is that she's not placing any demands on you. She's become your escape, and things just went too far and got way out of hand."

John says, "Yes, you're right, and now I don't know what to do. So that's why we're here."

"That was good," Lady Campbell says. "We're going to end it here, and we'll see you both in two weeks." They hug and thank them, and they leave.

John leaves the counseling session wanting to say something to Sheila as they both walk out of the church and head to their cars. But he just doesn't know what to say that would make her feel any better, so he says nothing, only looks at her a few times before he gets in his car and leaves.

John has a lot to think about as he makes his way back to his place. The challenge of having to face himself and come to terms with his issues of not having a father and how he handles being under pressure has caused him to feel uncomfortable, all while he continues to get calls from Jasmine. At this point, he thinks that he needs to stay away from her while he tries to sort through all of this and put things in its rightful place, including his relationship with her. He doesn't want to allow the sex with her to distort his thinking.

John, admits to himself for the first time that he is afraid. He sees what he has done to Sheila, his wife, and he doesn't know where to begin or how to help her, let alone himself. And with Jasmine still calling him he feels himself getting a little weak. He thinks, *Maybe I'll call her back so she can stop calling and see her just one more time.*

TEN

John calls Jasmine and asks if he can see her. "Yeah, come on over. Jacqueline is with her father for the weekend."

"Oh, so that means I can stay the weekend and have you to myself?"

Laughing, she says, "Yes, John, you can stay the weekend." But in her mind, she thinks, *You can stay forever.* Jasmine is lost in her thoughts as they hang up, for she's truly falling for him. When they're together she pretends that he's her husband. And now, since one of her dreams is about to come true, she wonders if all of her dreams concerning John will come true.

John hangs up, thinking that he's got it made. He has this beautiful woman, who has way more feelings for him than he has for her. But he does really like her a lot, and he knows that she wants more because she's not hiding her feelings for him. But John is not really playing her, he's just on the fence. He still loves his wife, but he's not sure if he's in love with her. He's confused. But right now, he's going to enjoy his time with Jasmine while it lasts.

He arrives at her house, duffle bag in hand and ready to stay for the weekend as he rings her doorbell. She opens it with a warm smile as she sees John, her husband for the weekend. She's so excited to see him with his bag that she kisses and hugs him before letting him in the house. Her mind is going a mile a minute, and she thinks she has to make this one of his best weekends. One he will not forget. She has plans for him, but first she's going to spoil him by catering to him, all in an attempt to allure his every sense. *I'm not trying to trap him, I just want him to see how it could be with me,* she thinks. She snaps out of it and takes his bag to let him in, then puts his bag on the steps leading upstairs. She turns around and offers him something to drink. "I went to the store when we hung up and I bought you some bottled beer. I put some in the freezer."

"You didn't have to do that but, I'll take one. Thanks."

She gets a fruit drink for herself and sits on the couch next to him. This is the first time she's talked to him since she started her new job, so she says, "Let me tell you about my new job. You know I'm an administrative assistant. I type up all the case reports that each of the investigators dictate. The cases are so interesting…they range from check fraud, spousal cheating, company embezzlement. They do it all and I get to read everything, and of course it's all confidential. There's only one woman there and she's the one who got me this job. I knew her from the dentist's office. Oh, and I forgot, I also handle the payments of services. And once I complete three months I get full benefits. They even offer a 401K plan, and they match it two percent."

"I'm happy for you, baby. This job seems to be a lot interesting and better. I believe that you'll become permanent," he says as he kisses her.

"Thanks, baby, for your support and your belief in me."

Jasmine treats John like a king the entire weekend. She feeds him in more ways than one, and he's very satisfied. She even gives him full body massages. She does whatever he asks her to do, or at least she tries her best to do, even in the bedroom.

John is beginning to feel a little like this is his castle and he's the king, because she makes him feel so good and comfortable as she caters to his every need. *Wow,* he thinks, *she's got me so relaxed and her massage really relieved my stress. Boy, I'll be crazy to leave all of this.* But Sheila keeps flashing in his mind.

But Jasmine has now become a new problem, which is making him even more confused. He knows he needs to slow things down with her so he can clear his head, get himself together and truly sort out his feelings towards Sheila, and towards Jasmine, before he even attempts to talk to her. He wonders how and why he's gotten himself into this situation.

It's 1:00 on Sunday afternoon, and John will be leaving around 4:00 so Jasmine can pick up her daughter from her mom's. John is feeling refreshed and revived, and he's sitting on the couch chilling while Jasmine is in the kitchen fixing dinner before he leaves. John contemplates how he's going to tell her they need to slow things down so he can sort some things out. He's really enjoyed a weekend of playing house, but he knows that he has a real house—the one he left broken. He has to determine whether he wants to try to fix it, if it's fixable, because he does still love Sheila. He knows it's all his fault, but sometimes once you lose it you can never get it back.

And then there's Jasmine, this spicy spitfire cracker of a woman who has a child, something Sheila wants so desperately to have with him but he'd made her stay on the pill. It dawns on him that Jasmine once said she was on the pill, but he never asked her if she's still on it. *She's got to be…she knows my situation,* he thinks—and that if she isn't on the pill and has gotten pregnant, how much more complicated she would make an already complicated situation.

Jasmine has been calling John for three weeks now and he hasn't returned any of her calls, leaving her wondering what has happened. Their weekend had been perfect, so she doesn't understand what's going on. Then she thinks could it be his wife, and her attitude changes. *I love him and I'm not giving him up not without a fight,* she thinks. *He has to be mine. I don't do the things she does. I know how to make him happy. I deserve a chance for true love. I'm a good person. I want a man to call my own.*

Tears begin to flow as she thinks about her life. She thinks about how much she hates that she was taught at a young age to use her good looks and her body to get what she wants out of life. She thinks about the toxic relationship she had with Paul, her ex, and all the men she used in between. *Look at me, it got me nowhere. I'm sitting here crying over a man that's not mine, and I don't want to give him up. He's the best thing that's ever happened to me. He's a real good, honest man, even though he didn't tell me he was married right from the start. I would have never thought that our innocent hellos would have developed into a serious relationship. It all just happened. We didn't plan on this happening.* To her, John is different, because she's watched him struggle within their relationship. *I can't lose him, I just can't.*

Two more weeks go by and she still hasn't heard from John, though she calls several times and leaves messages. She starts feeling a little funny in her stomach, thinking it's perhaps her nerves or maybe some type of virus that will soon pass.

John has just realized how much all of this has affected him, not just emotionally but physically as well, for he's poured himself into each woman.

It's John's vacation time and he surely needs it. He shuts himself in his apartment for three weeks, relaxing, sleeping and really thinking about his situation. Thinking about Sheila, he looks at her as being this beautiful but needy, clingy woman, one who's not a risk taker. Though she's very smart, she lacks self-esteem and confidence. She supports him, even though he feels like she needs to get a life. And then there's Jasmine, also beautiful, a feisty woman— the total opposite of Sheila. She speaks her mind and don't take no stuff. She has confidence and she's a risk taker. Though John gets along well with her, she has a child, something he doesn't want right now.

He has to decide if he's willing to throw away ten years of marriage and if it's worth reuniting to rebuild their marriage, or should he go for someone new who has a child, which means he has to deal with the father—a life that would be unpredictable and possibly full of drama because he hasn't known Jasmine very long, someone with which he has no history. Then he starts thinking about his likes and dislikes. When it comes to Sheila, he likes how she supports him. She always has his back, and she is consistent, steady, and reliable. He dislikes her pressuring him about having a child, her nagging, and her lack of self-esteem and confidence. For Jasmine, he likes how she treats him like a king, how she has ideas for his side business, and that she's encouraging and a good listener. He likes her confidence and feistiness. He dislikes her strong forcefulness and cunning ways, and how she easily uses her looks and body to get what she wants, as if she has no self-esteem or self-worth. It seems as if she feels that's all she has to offer anyone, and that she better get what she can while she can.

John is feeling lost and confused. He truly doesn't know what to do. And before he knows it, he hears himself praying. *God, I need your help right now. I know it's been awhile for me and I'm sorry. But God, I'm at a loss here, and I need you to lead and guide me in making the right choice, your choice. Lord, please see me and hear my cry. In Jesus' name I pray, amen.* He doesn't realize it, but he's also crying; he feels overwhelmed and can't stop himself. He's caught up in something he never meant to happen.

Jasmine still hasn't heard from John, and she's a nervous wreck. It's been over a month since their last encounter and she really misses him. Her stomach has not settled down and now she's getting sick in the mornings. She's called out twice from work because of it, but she goes to work today because she needs to. She's a little better but still not feeling herself.

Sheila goes to see how Jasmine feels and just talk with her. She walks up to Jasmine just as she's hanging up the phone. "So how are you feeling?"

"I'm here but I'm not myself."

"What's wrong?"

"My stomach's been bothering me, and now I'm vomiting. And I've haven't heard from my man in over a month. And you ask me what's wrong?" Tears well up in her eyes.

"Wow," Sheila says. "I'm sorry. Have you called the doctor? Maybe you have a stomach virus. Or could you be pregnant?"

"Pregnant? Oh my god, I never thought about that. What if I am? What will I do? He's not returning my calls. I just hung up from calling him again when you walked up."

"What happened? Did y'all have a fight?"

"No, that's the thing. He stayed at my place for the weekend and we had a wonderful time but I haven't heard from him since."

"Maybe he didn't have a wonderful time," Sheila suggests.

"Oh, he did. I catered to him and treated him like a king."

"Well, could he have someone else?"

"That's what I'm afraid of," Jasmine says as her tears fall again. "I really love him and I know he has strong feelings for me."

"Well, the first thing you need to do is go to the doctor, see if you have a virus or if you're pregnant. Then you need to go after your man. Wait for him at his job or go to his house. That is, if you know where he works or lives at."

"Yeah, but he moved into an apartment and I don't know the number."

"That's all right. You can go there and park where

you can see him pulling in and wait. You know, do your own stakeout and make him talk to you."

"You're right, if he won't talk to me I'll make him even if I have to cause a scene. Thanks, I'll get to the bottom of this."

"Trust me," Sheila says, "I know men can sometimes be that blessing and that curse."

"Oh, girl, I know that's right," Jasmine answers. They almost high-five each other, because for a quick second they almost forget where they're at.

Sheila clears her throat. "Make that appointment today and let me know."

"I'll do it now," Jasmine says, and makes a doctor's appointment for the following week.

Jasmine's at her doctor's appointment and she's a little nervous. The nurse takes her blood pressure and asks about the nature of her visit. Jasmine tells her that she's been having issues with her stomach.

The nurse makes notes. "Ok, the doctor will be in shortly."

"Shortly" was more like 20 minutes. When the doctor finally comes in, she says, "So I see here you're having some stomach issues." She tells Jasmine to sit on the table so she can examine her and check her stomach out, then asked a few questions.

Jasmine asks, "Is there some type of stomach virus going around?"

"There is, but it only lasts for 24 to 48 hours. You said it's been two weeks." The doctor suggests they do a pregnancy test.

Jasmine agrees. The doctor goes out and the nurse comes back in to draw her blood. About 15 minutes later the doctor comes back. "Well, you're pregnant."

"I'm what! How far??"

"It looks like about seven weeks."

"What? That's almost two months."

"Yes, but an ultrasound can be a little more accurate, so I need you to set up an appointment." Jasmine agrees to the ultrasound.

By the next day, Jasmine goes to work with mixed feelings. Part of her is excited because she loves John and believes that this baby might make him come around and seal their union. But the other part of her is afraid, because they never got far enough in their relationship to talk about kids, even though she knows he likes her daughter.

Sheila's had a busy morning, but now that it's quieted down she goes and checks up on Jasmine. Not wasting small talk, she says, "What did the doctor say?"

"I'm two months pregnant."

"Ok...how you feel about it?"

"I'm happy and afraid."

Sheila says, "Does he know?"

"I'm planning on staking his place out tonight."

"Be prepared to wait it out."

Jasmine says, "I'm afraid of his reaction. But I have to let him know I didn't plan this pregnancy. I don't want him to think I was trying to trick him. I have a three-year-old daughter and a baby daddy. I really don't want another baby daddy. For once, I want a man who truly loves me."

"Do you know his schedule?"

"His schedule?"

"Yeah, most people have a routine, a pattern in what they do. You know, like you leave work, drive the same route, get home at the same time, a pattern."

"Oh yeah, he gets off at 5:00 and he usually calls me about 5:30 or 6:00."

"Ok, so this is what you do. I'll cover for you so you can leave an hour and a half early. You get yourself together so you can be at his place before 5:30, and you must park somewhere near the entrance where you can watch for him."

"Are you sure?" Jasmine asks, tears in her eyes.

Sheila is tearing up too as she says, "Yeah, there's a baby involved here." A tear slips away and slides down her face. "All I ever wanted was to have a baby."

"But Sheila, you're not old…you still can."

"Not when your husband is cheating on you," Sheila says, tears still falling down her face.

"I'm so sorry, Sheila."

"Thanks, but people are going to do what they want to do. They don't try to put themselves in that wife's or girlfriend's shoes. And yeah, I know it's the guys fault too, because he knows he has a wife or a girlfriend." She looks at Jasmine. "You tell me you want a man who truly loves you? Girl, please."

"Sheila, I really am sorry. And yes, I do."

"Yeah I know, I'm sorry too. Now you better get out of here."

At work the next day, Jasmine is still upset, and Sheila comes over to her desk. "What happened? Did you confront him?"

"No. I was at his apartment before he got off of work and I waited for two hours but he never showed up." Jasmine begins to cry. "I don't know if I can do this."

"Oh no, girl we're not giving up. There's a baby

involved now and he has to know it. So this is what we're going to do: I'm going with you and we're going to find him, no matter how long it takes."

Jasmine comes from around her desk and hugs Sheila. "Oh, thank you. I'm a nervous wreck. I still don't know what I'm going to say to him."

"Well, I'll help you figure that out, and I'm here to give you that moral support. Now we can go today since it's been slow. I'll check to see if we both can leave an hour early. I'm sure it's fine. So we can go home and put on something comfortable, go to the bathroom, and grab some stuff because we'll be waiting awhile. I'll meet you say, what, at his place? Give me his address and I'll hop in your car and we'll wait." As Jasmine gives her the address, Sheila can't help thinking that John lives in the same apartment complex.

As they sit in Jasmine's car, they talk while they wait. Jasmine asks Sheila, "What do I say?"

"Tell him you miss him and that since he hasn't been returning your calls you decided to come to see him."

"Yeah, it's the truth. I'm going to say that."

A car pulls in, and they both look. "It's not him," Jasmine says. They've been waiting already about 35 minutes. "What if he tries to ignore me?"

"Then you make him listen."

"But how?"

"Ok girl, if he starts to walk away or tries to get loud on you, drop that bomb and tell him you're pregnant. That will shut him up and stop him in his tracks."

About fifteen minutes later, another car pulls in and they both look now. Sheila thinks that that looks like John's truck as it passes on Sheila's side, and both she and Jasmine speak at the same time.

"John."

Jasmine says, "That's him."

And then they both look at each other.

They both rush to jump out of the car, walking towards John before he's finished parking. John pulls into a parking spot, turns off the car and hops out, hitting his alarm. He starts to walk away, then surprisingly sees Sheila and then Jasmine coming toward him. He looks at them both, thinking, *This can't be happening. How did they find out about each other?*

Sheila steps right in his face and slaps him. "I just want to know why. How could you do this to me? Was going to counseling saying you wanted our marriage to work a lie too?"

"What? Sheila, no! I admitted to you that I was seeing someone and it kind of just happened, but I haven't talked to her in weeks. And yes, I was trying to see if we can work things out. But why are you trying to set me up? How long have you two known about each other? And now y'all trying to play games? Let me guess, this was her idea?"

"Oh ok, first of all, I'm not a 'her' now," Jasmine says. "And that's why you haven't been returning my calls? So you was just going to walk away from me just like that, huh? Let me tell you something, you can't play with people's feelings like that. You come and stay with me a few weekends, knowing how I feel about you?"

"Look, Jasmine, I'm so sorry. I didn't mean for all this to happen, it all happened so fast. And I do have feelings for you."

"Yeah, whatever, John. And you show me that by

what, trying to see if you could work things out with your wife? And I thought you were different. So let me guess, if it didn't work out you were going to come back to me? Wow. Oh, let me answer your questions. First of all, this wasn't no set up or my idea. Sheila was helping me to confront my man, but what we didn't know was that we're both in love with the same man. And you see John, your wife was the woman I exchanged numbers with when I was afraid I was going to lose my job. She was a patient at the dentist's office I used to work at. She's the one that got me this job at Smith & Gilford Investigators. So that's how I know Sheila, and I just found out that she's your wife. We became quite close. And one more thing John, since you say you have feelings for me, does that include our baby? Yeah, I'm two months pregnant."

ELEVEN

Traci comes home from her meeting with Lady Campbell with mixed feelings. She's glad to realize that some of her feelings for Paul comes out of a need for what she's lacking with Steven, but she can't explain the reason why she was attracted to Paul when she was a dancer before she even met her husband. And it doesn't change the fact that she has these feelings now.

Traci appreciates Lady Campbell's help, but in her mind she feels it's to no avail—Paul is still in the forefront of her mind. She thinks about him every day and would love to see him again, even though it would be the first time since their little confessions to one another. She doesn't want to do anything with him; she just enjoys him and their conversations. She can't resist, so she finally calls him. The phone rings three times, and he answers on the fourth.

"Hello?" he says, sounding a little winded.

"Hey, did I catch you at a bad time? I'm sorry, you can call me back if you like."

"Oh no, it's fine. I just came out of the shower and I heard the phone ringing. I'm glad you called me, because I've been thinking about you a lot lately."

"Oh you have, have you?" she says playfully. "Well, I've been thinking about you and that's why I called."

"When can you get away so we can spend some time together?"

"My son is at day care and I won't have to pick him up until a few hours from now. So I'm free now, how about you?"

"Yeah I'm free. Just give me 20 minutes to put something on. Where should I meet you?"

"At the restaurant in the next town, if you remember how to get there. Or at the market and you can follow me again."

"I would love to follow you, but yeah, at the market's good. I'll call you back when I'm ready and we can leave out then."

"Ok, I'll be waiting for your call."

Paul is excited that Traci called. To him, it means that she does have feelings for him and that she's opened the door of possibilities and opportunities. He hangs up, rushing around his bedroom trying to find something nice and neat to wear. He's glad he freshly shaved.

After getting ready, he calls Traci saying he's about to leave out. He doesn't want to waste any more time, because he needs to see her. When he gets to the market, she's already there and he follows her to their restaurant.

Walking into the restaurant, Traci is nervous but

also filled with excitement to see him. They see their table is empty so they ask to be seated there. After ordering drinks and something to eat, they sit there for a few minutes, gazing at each other. "I must tell you, I can't stop thinking about you," Traci finally says.

"I know the feeling. I can't stop thinking about you, either."

Traci confesses that she's spoken to her pastor's wife about her feelings. "Oh?" he says, raising his eyebrows in surprise. "So, what did she say?"

"I don't think she really helped me, but she did help me realize that I've been feeling neglected and lonely because my husband doesn't have time for me. You see, he's a minister at my church. He wasn't when I met him, but later he felt God's calling and he answered it. And in doing so, my son and I became left out. I know he has to do what he has to do for God, but he has to learn how to balance his time. The pastor's wife tried to point out that you're just temporarily filling this void I have. But I think it's more than that, because I was attracted to you when I was dancing. You were different."

"That's because *you're* different," he says, staring at her intently. "Dancing was something you did; it's not who you are."

Traci's heart leaps. "That's why I really like you."

Their food comes, and they eat and talk some more. "You know, it meant a lot to me that you called me," Paul says. "I want to kiss you right now…badly." His comment causes her to blush. She doesn't realize she's speaking out loud as she says that she's been wanting to kiss him, too.

Paul sits with a big grin on his face. "Oh, you're

full of surprises."

"Why do you say that?"

"Well, you just told me you've been wanting to kiss me too."

"What? I did? Oh, how embarrassing. I thought I was just thinking it."

"No, you weren't, and I'm glad you feel the same way. What are we going to do?" he asks as he reaches for her hand.

She slowly glides her hand toward his. Their fingers touch playfully before they intertwine, as if they embraced and are locked within each other. "Are you finished? Are you ready to go?" Paul says. "Because we need to get this kiss out of the way."

"Yeah, I'm done, we can go."

"Is there a park nearby so we can be alone?" he asks once they're out in the parking lot. She says yes, and he follows her to the park. She gets out of her car and into his. He can't wait for her to get in the car before he reaches over to kiss her. She kisses him back. They both feel the sparks that they've seemed to generate, and it takes a minute before they come up for some air. When they do, they're both hot and bothered and speechlessly lost in their own thoughts.

Paul speaks first. "Wow…your lips are so soft, just like I thought they were. And your kisses are so good. I want more, but that will have to do for now. Please don't make me wait too long to get some more."

"Your kisses are good, as well," Traci says. "And I know I shouldn't be here with you doing this, but we have this chemistry that's drawing me to you." She leans towards him for another kiss, which ends up being equally as long as the first but with more passion. "I have to go."

"When can I see you again? I don't know what you're doing to me, but I have to see you again."

Traci says, "Oh, Paul. I feel the same way. I'm so confused. This is wrong…I'm married."

"I know. And I really don't mean to cause you pain or confusion, but we can't help how we feel about each other."

"Yeah, that's true, but it's still wrong." She moves to get out of the car but he grabs her hand.

"Wait a minute." He gets out of the car to open her door, extending his hand. She takes it and gets out. Still holding her hand, he pulls her close and holds tight, saying nothing. He holds her close for a few minutes before finally letting her go.

"Thank you, I feel better now," Traci says. "I'll call you later."

Traci meets up with Paul at their favorite spot. They ask for their favorite booth, because it's empty.

He starts by telling her how much he's missed her and how she's always on his mind. "This is crazy. I can't stop thinking about you too," Traci says.

He stares at her seriously. "I don't mean to make things hard for you, but I can't help how I feel. I want you, Traci. Can we go to a hotel? I won't do anything that you won't let me do." They pay their bill, and of course, since Paul doesn't know his way around he has to follow her.

They go two more towns over to the Hilton Hotel. They're both nervous and they check into Room 209. Traci goes into the bathroom. She's already used it but she also wants to try to get a handle on her nerves.

Paul also uses the bathroom, and when he comes

out he immediately takes off his clothes and gets into bed. Traci watches him as he strips off his clothes and gets into bed, waiting for her. She had been expecting some kissing or something before they get into the bed, so she removes her own clothes. She hears him say, "Hmm," as she comes around the bed to get in while he follows her with his eyes.

He pulls the covers back for her to get in, and he doesn't wait for her to get settled in before he turns to fondle her breast and kisses her deeply. It takes a few minutes for her nerves to settle down before she starts to respond, and she gives herself to him as their passion takes control. Afterwards, they take separate showers and both use her lotion.

While putting on lotion, Paul asks her if she's ok. "Yes, I'm ok. What we just did I wanted to happen, and I know I have to deal with the consequences. But right now I feel a little guilty and yet happy at the same time."

"Yeah, I feel the same way," Paul says, "but I don't want to stop seeing you. Your kisses do something to me." As he gets dressed before leaving the room, he says, "Tell me I'll see you again."

"Yes, you'll see me again."

They leave the hotel, walk to their cars, and he follows her until they get into their town where he's familiar, then he goes his own way.

When Traci gets home, her husband, Steven, is in the kitchen. She had wanted to beat him home.

For some reason, now of all times he wants to hug and kiss her. Most of the time he shows little affection, though he used to all the time. She squirms playfully away, trying not to get him suspicious. She doesn't want him to smell the hotel soap. "What's gotten into you?"

"Nothing's gotten into me. I just want to hug and kiss you, that's all. Why, is something wrong with that?"

"Oh no, of course not. I've just gotten used to you not doing those types of things anymore."

"Come on now, what kind of thing is that to say?"

I don't want to have this conversation with him, she thinks. She just says, "Well, we both have been so busy with our own stuff, that's all." She doesn't want to say too much to make him want to change things, at least not now, because she's so caught up into Paul.

"We have been busy, and now that Pastor has me going out to see the sick I'm not home as much."

"What can I say about it? You're doing the Lord's work."

Steven walks over to kiss her full on the mouth. "Thanks for being so understanding."

"No problem, baby."

Traci comes home feeling good, for she anticipates seeing Paul. Steven had called earlier and told her that he was going to take Steven Jr. to his mom's for the weekend so Traci could have some time to herself, and he may be doing that twice a month depending on how this weekend works out for her. *Why is he doing this?* she wonders. Then she remembers their conversation two weeks ago and realizes that that's where this is coming from. It makes her feel bad, because her first thought is that she can spend more time with Paul now. She calls Paul and tells him what's going on and that she can't see him that day, just in case Steven has plans in mind.

In two days, it will be the second weekend since she told Paul she couldn't see him. During that time, Steven stayed home four weeknights. Now Traci is more than ready to see Paul, so they plan to meet on Saturday. Traci will meet him at the hotel and Paul will get there early to tell her the room number.

It's Saturday and Steven is still at home, putting around. Traci can't help but have an attitude, wondering to herself why he is still home. She wants to ask him but she doesn't want to alert him.

Steven has been feeling that something is going on with Traci. He's caught her a few times talking secretly on the phone. At times, she seems to be lost in a daze, and he has to call her several times before she answers him. He wonders if she's cheating on him. *I know I haven't been giving her help with Steven Jr. and I haven't been spending any time with her,* he thinks. *But I want to believe that if we were in trouble and she's not happy that she would tell me, complain, or do something, but she hasn't. I don't know what's going on, but I'm going to find out.*

Traci still plans on sticking to her plans with Paul. She sneaks into the bathroom with her cell phone and texts him that Steven hasn't left yet and she's hoping he leaves soon so she can leave. Paul texts back, "Ok, just be careful." She replies, "Ok, I will."

It takes another half an hour before Steven finally leaves, and Traci takes another 20 minutes before leaving herself just in case he comes back. She makes it out with no sighting, and as she drives along to meet Paul she has an uneasy feeling, though she continues on because she needs to see him. She cautiously keeps looking at her rearview mirror to see if she spots her husband following her. She nervously approaches the hotel and she calls Paul to let him know she's there and how she feels uneasy.

"Ok, circle around before you come up," he says. "I can see you. If I see anything I'll tell you." She circles around, and before she pulls into the lot she gets out the car to look around herself before going inside.

Once inside the room, she lets out a sigh of relief. It takes her about 20 minutes before she's able to relax. "I think Steven suspects something…I'm not sure," she says. "He never just putts around the house; he's always up and out." She looks at Paul. "What if he really was following me?"

"I'm not scared of him."

"I know, but he does have a temper."

Paul laughs. "Oh, but you haven't seen mine. Maybe he'll meet his match."

"Oh Paul, don't talk like that."

"Look Traci, I'm not playing no games with you. My feelings for you are real and I would fight for you. I'm not letting you go. I love you."

Her eyes fill with tears as she looks at him. "I'm falling for you too, but I can't be. This isn't right." Paul grabs and holds her. "Everything will work out the way it's supposed to." He kisses her, first gently and then again with all the passion he has within. Soon they're tearing off each other's clothes until they stand before each other naked, gazing with desire at each other. When Paul takes her to bed, it's altogether different and beautiful. Their lovemaking is beautiful as, uninhibited, they both freely give themselves to each other.

Traci and Paul walk out the hotel door holding hands. The residue of their love blissfully shines on them until they get to Traci's car, and they lean against it for one last kiss before they part.

Steven suddenly jumps out of his car, fists balled and ready to fight. He's parked close enough to the hotel entrance but not close enough to be seen by Traci and Paul. He starts walking, then his walk becomes a jog and he begins running hard when he sees them kissing. "Traci!" he hollers. She turns just as Steven swings a raging punch, grazing Paul on the side of his face.

Paul pushes Traci aside and braces himself for whatever Steven wants to do. Traci, however, knows what Steven is about to do. "Steven! Please no. I'm sorry." He looks at her and she sees his every emotion.

Steven looks back at Paul. "This is my wife. Did she tell you she's married or do you just don't care? Oh, I'm going to see you again, trust me."

Traci arrives home, and Steven comes home behind her. She's afraid of what he may do. Even though Steven has never harmed her, he does have a bad temper and she's afraid that this might have pushed him over the edge. She remains quiet, not saying a word as she waits on him to start the conversation.

Steven says, "How long, Traci, has this been going on?"

"Two months, but it's really been about four months."

"When did it become intimate?"

"Just this month, but it been the last two months." By this point, Traci is crying. "Steven, I'm so sorry."

"Traci, how could you do this?"

"Steven, it's like I said before, you're too busy.

119

You never have time for me," Traci says, still crying. "We don't do any of the things we used to do, now especially since you became a minister. I don't even know how to say this," she says as she breaks down, "but it stole you away from me. How do you compete with God? You can't." She calms down and adds, "You haven't been married to me for a long while."

"Traci, why didn't you say anything?"

"What's there to say? It's like you have another woman that you're crazy about and would do anything to keep her happy. You just forgot about me, and I just became your son's mother, not your wife. So, what's there to say? What, tell you to choose between me and him? I didn't sign up for all of this, you did. I would never say that, and that would look like you're married to a non-believer. I believe in God. I believe that his son, Jesus Christ, died on the cross for my sins. And I know that without him I'll be nothing. You see, I know God and I love him." Tears stream down her cheeks. "I'm just not as committed as you are. I carry him with me too, so don't judge me because I don't worship like you do. He's in my heart." Tears in her eyes, she stands there feeling guilty for her feelings.

"Traci, I'm so sorry, I had no idea you felt this way. I guess things kind of changed quickly for me once I accepted my calling as a minister. And I have neglected you, I'm sorry. I didn't mean to, it's just that being a part of the ministry is so exciting. I just got so caught up into ministering to God's people. I know I'm not preaching, I did do my trial sermon a while ago. I have to do what Pastor says, go wherever my help is needed, and right now it's ministering to the sick. For me, it's like what Jesus did. Traci, I don't want you to feel that you have to compete, but I wish you would have told me your feelings." He looks at her. "How do we get past this?"

"I don't know," she answers, and things seem to calm down between them. Traci is a little hopeful until he says, "I just have to know where you met him at."

Traci's heart drops. She doesn't want to lie to him any longer, so she tells the truth. "I met him years ago when I was a stripper."

"What? You kept in contact with him?"

"Oh no, he's new to this neighborhood and he happened to run into me one day and we got caught up briefly."

"So, you're telling me this dude was one of your old patrons who watched you dance and now after all this time you see him again and now you're sleeping with him? You just don't sleep with someone unless you have some type of feelings for them, so you have feelings for him."

Traci pauses before answering. "Yes, I've danced for him and yes, I did like him, we had good conversations. He was different from the others."

Steven is really fuming now. "It's not just the fact that you're sleeping with him." His voice gets louder. "I told you years ago guys who go to those places fantasize about being with you, especially when they see you on the street. And you already know how I feel about that."

"No Steven, please don't go there."

"You're taking me there. And you better not see this guy or talk to him again."

"I know," she says, only hoping he can control herself.

Paul is furious as he gets into his car, but he wants to make sure Traci is okay, and figures that by following her he'll also learn where she lives at. He pulls off, spots her car, and sees her husband following her, so he lets another car get in front of him as he slowly follows behind them.

When Traci pulls into the driveway of her house, Steven parks beside her. Paul stops at the corner and watches them go into the house. He pulls up and parks, having full view of their house. He sits there for a while, watching the house and their cars, thinking that now he knows what her husband's car looks like. Suddenly the front door opens and her husband comes out, gets into his car, and pulls off. Paul quickly ducks down in his seat as he drives past him, then he sits up and looks around. Finally, he calls Traci.

Traci answers the phone. "Paul, are you ok?"

"Yeah, are you ok? I'm out front. I followed you to make sure you're ok."

"Yeah, he wanted to know how I know you. I told him I knew you from my past and we were talking for about two months and we became intimate just this month."

"Where'd he go?"

"He had to go to the hospital to visit a couple of church members, so he'll be gone for a little bit. But I know he'll be calling to check up on me."

"And you'll be home to answer his call. Baby, let me in. I need to see that you're ok."

She lets out a big sigh. "Come around back. I'm in the kitchen."

Paul walks in the house, looks around, then grabs

Traci to make sure she's ok. He kisses her passionately. She pulls away. "Paul, we have to stop…you can't be here. I don't know when he'll be back."

"I know, but promise me you'll see me again soon." He grabs her shoulders and looks directly in her eyes. "Traci, I'm in love with you and I'm not giving you up. I'll fight for you; do you hear me?"

Traci is alarmed by his grip. His words are passionate and almost frightening, but she says, "I know."

He holds her close to his heart, which seems to calm her down. He kisses her one more time before he leaves.

In the middle of Traci and Steven's conversation, Steven phone rings. It's Pastor Campbell, asking him if he could go see Brother Johnson at the hospital. "Yes, I'll be there in about 15 minutes," Steven says.

"Good, thank you," Pastor replies before hanging up.

"I know, you have to go," Traci says.

Steven looks at her. "Yeah, it's—"

Traci cuts him off. "I know, Pastor of course. How would I have ever guessed?"

"Come on Traci, I shouldn't be longer than an hour. And we can finish this when I come back." Traci has mixed feelings. She's happy he's leaving because he was becoming angry when she told him where she met Paul, and yet she's sad because once again he's leaving her.

Steven gets in his car, still a little angry but trying to calm down before he gets to the hospital. He wants his mind right before he prays for Brother Johnson, so he starts to pray for himself. He's good by the time he gets to the hospital, ready to minister to the sick.

He does what he needs to do and leaves, but on his way home his thoughts go right back to this other guy and his anger starts to rebuild. And now all his old feelings about Traci's dancing are really resurfacing. He doesn't know who he's angrier at, her or himself. He realizes now how he slipped up and neglected her, and he's not quite sure if he can handle this.

He's about to pull up to his house when he sees this guy quickly getting into his car and pulling off. His first thought is to follow him, but he tells himself to stop it, your acting paranoid, so he just pulls into the driveway.

Traci has just come out of the bathroom after taking a shower. She hears the front door opening, and she hurries to throw on her pajamas and goes downstairs. She goes into the kitchen, but Steven isn't there. He'd heard her moving around, but he was too hurt and angry at them both to say anything. Traci knows he's in the basement since he's not in the kitchen. She starts to go down to see him but stops, deciding to give him his space. She goes back upstairs, secretly wishing that she would fall asleep before he comes upstairs. She doesn't know how to handle his temper, especially when it's directed towards her. She lays in bed and tries to fall asleep, but her thoughts turn to Paul, not Steven.

Meanwhile, Steven is in the basement, contemplating his next move. He's determined now to get this guy one way or the other. He tries to relax, but his mind won't let him. He feels the old Steven creeping up. *I have to get a handle on myself and this situation before everything gets out of control,* he thinks. But when he closes his eyes, all he sees are images of Traci and this guy. *I can't even touch her,* he thinks, beginning to cry.

Steven remains in the basement for hours, the TV on though he isn't watching it. It takes a while, but he finally falls asleep.

The next morning, Traci awakens feeling emotionally drained and calls out of work. Seeing that Steven never came to bed, she lays there until Steven comes in the room 20 minutes later. They speak, but she notices a change in him, one that she can see in his eyes. It gives Traci a chill. He doesn't have anything to say to her, just goes into the bathroom, takes his shower, then gets dressed and leaves her still in the bed. Traci is so upset that she needs to talk to someone, so she calls Sheila.

Sheila is in her office trying to work, but she can't focus. She's about to leave because she came in early. As her cell phone rings, she looks at the screen and sees it's Traci. "Hello?"

"Hi Sheila, are you busy?"

"No, just about to leave the office. What's up?"

Traci starts talking quickly until Sheila says, "Steven? Paul? What? Traci, start over and slow down. First of all, where are you?"

"Home. I just couldn't go to work today."

"Ok, I'll be there in about half an hour."

Traci starts crying. "Ok. Steven's not home."

They hang up, and Sheila leaves the office, worried about Traci. She gets in her car and heads to Traci's house. When she arrives, they sit in the kitchen and talk. Traci tells her how Steven caught her and Paul coming out of the hotel and that Steven swung and grazed Paul's cheek but he swayed to the side. She mentions how she and Steven had talked but now this morning he seemed to be distant and that he had changed. "Sheila, I'm scared. Paul followed me home yesterday and when Steven went out Paul came knocking on the door. I know I should have told him to leave but I told him to go around to the back door. He wanted to make sure I was ok. I didn't tell you, but he told me he's loves me and he'll fight for me."

"What? Girl, oh, you got some stuff on your hands."

"I know," Traci says, still crying.

Sheila gets up and hugs her as she cries herself. "What a mess we're both in." She tells Traci what's going on in her situation.

Traci is glad their counseling session is tomorrow because Steven hasn't come back to their bedroom yet. She's been tiptoeing around him because she's not sure where they stand.

Steven comes home early that night while Traci is in the kitchen finishing up dinner and Steven Jr. is in the living room watching cartoons. He walks in and hugs and talks with Little Steven about his day, then goes into the kitchen. "Hi."

"Hi," Traci answers. "Dinner's almost ready."

"Oh, I ate already."

"Well you at least could have called me. I wouldn't have fixed all of this." Steven doesn't respond, but walks away and heads downstairs.

Traci fights the urge to follow him and give him a piece of her mind, but since their son is in the other room she doesn't want him to hear them arguing. She and Little Steven eat, then she cleans up and they go upstairs. After putting him to bed, she goes into her room. Still upset with Steven she hopes tomorrow's session will help put their marriage back on track.

The next day, Steven wakes up and comes upstairs to take a shower. Traci is up when he comes out of the bathroom. "Hi," is all he says.

"Hi," she answers in an unsure tone.

"I'm taking Little Steven to my mom's. What time is the session?"

"It's at 11 o'clock."

"Ok, I'll see you there." He leaves to go get Little Steven ready.

Wow, he's really upset with all of this, Traci thinks as she gets up and starts to prepare herself for the day. *I should have told him how I felt before. I hope we can work this out.*

Later, Steven pulls up to the church to look for Traci's car but she's not there yet. When Traci does arrive she sees Steven's car, and she parks near him, gets out and walks toward his car. Steven gets out and waits for her, then they walk towards the church. Someone calls out Traci's name, and they stop and turn to see Paul approaching them. Steven walks toward Paul with his fists drawn, ready to fight. Traci looks in shock at Paul.

"Look man, no disrespect to you but I'm in love with your wife," Paul says.

"You what!" Steven yells, and swings a hard right at him.

127

TWELVE

John feels as if he's been punched in the chest and had the wind knocked out of him. He stumbles backwards against someone's car, for his knees have buckled from underneath him after Jasmine, his mistress's, words hit him: *I am pregnant, I'm two months.* Hearing her words takes him off guard and he doesn't hear anything else she says, for suddenly his mind goes blank for a few seconds. He quickly recovers and tries not to show any emotion, especially in front of his wife, Sheila, so his only defense is to get mad and try to shift the focus on him being set up. But in his head, he's scared of the fact that Sheila and Jasmine do know each other. Suddenly John breaks out in a sweat, his heart starts to beat faster and he can feel himself starting to panic. Looking around, he thinks, *I got to get out of here.* He turns and walks back to his car without saying a word.

Sheila is right on his heels. "Oh no John, you are

not getting away with this that easy!"

Hitting the alarm, he quickly gets in and starts the engine. Sheila bangs on the passenger's window. "Open the door!" He unlocks the door. She gets in and they pull off, leaving Jasmine behind.

Lost in his own head, John drives around aimlessly before he finally pulls over in the middle of a block filled with row houses. He looks around. The block is quiet and looks decent. It's a wide block, with more row houses across the street. He parks the car and turns off the engine, then leans his head against the head rest and closes his eyes. He sits there, almost forgetting that Sheila is there, too.

Sheila sits quietly, then finally speaks as her tears of hurt and anger flow. "Why did you let it go this far? You could have stopped this."

With eyes still closed, he says, "It all just happened. I told you that."

"So, what happens now since you have a baby on the way?"

"Look Sheila, I drove here to think and you wanted to hop in the car with me, claiming that I'm not getting away with this." For the first time, John looks at Sheila. "I really do not know." He rubs his head and forehead.

"Does she have your heart? Do you love her?"

"Sheila," John says, his voice rising a little, "I told you before *no*! But I do have feelings for her."

"I have loved you so much, all I ever wanted was to have your baby. Now someone else is giving you what should be ours. I should be the one carrying your child, John. It should be me," Sheila says, and breaks down crying. Then, trying to pull herself together, she adds, "Do you know how badly this hurts me? Do you know, John?" Her voice is rising. "I first go from hearing a message of you telling a woman that 'you know what I want, I want you,' when I didn't know you we're cheating on me to now knowing that that woman—my receptionist of all things—is now pregnant. And to think you wanted to keep me on the pill! I don't get it. Oh my God!" Sheila is struck with a sudden thought. "Was it me you just you didn't want to have a child with? John, was it me?" She points to herself as thoughts come to her mind. "You always told me it wasn't the right time or we weren't financially ready to have a child right now. And here you go and have an affair and she gets pregnant. You never gave me a chance…it was always about what you wanted. Never did you once care enough about me and what I wanted or my needs. It was always about you. I don't know, I…I…I can't handle this. I don't know, there's nothing else for me to say." Her tears constantly fall down her face as the reality of things sink in. She suddenly starts to get mad and begins to hit on him, yelling. "I gave you the best of me and this is what you give me!" She hits and shoves him as her anger erupts for a few seconds. She finally stops, feeling nothing but exhaustion. In a low voice, with her head turned looking out the window as she silently cries, she says, "Just take me back to your place so I can get my car."

John sits there, still with his hands protecting his face after he let her hit on him. "Oh, Sheila, I know I messed up and I am so sorry for causing you all this pain. If I could do it all over again none of this would be happening. Please, just give me some time."

"I just do not know, John; you broke our vows, my trust and my heart."

"I know, I know. Do not give up yet. Please tell me you won't give up yet. It's like what you always tell me, remember: if it's meant to be, true love will always find its way back."

"Yeah, well, that wasn't including someone else carrying your baby." John sighs deeply, then starts the car and heads back to his place. They are both silent, Sheila too broken to speak and John too afraid.

When they arrive at his place, Sheila rushes out of the car without saying a word. John sits there lost in his thoughts, trying to figure out what just happened here. "This is too much," he says out loud. "I can't deal with this...I need a drink to settle myself down." He starts the car and finds the nearest bar.

John sits down at the counter. "What would you like?" asks the bartender.

John looks up at him. "Give me something strong because I'm feeling a lot of stress and pressure and I need to settle myself down." John is not thinking about the fact he never drank before, only that he wants to numb his feelings and just clear his head of all of this.

"Okay buddy, I got something for you." The bartender pours him a doubt shot of gin on ice.

John picks it up and gulps it down, immediately feeling it burn. He puts his hand up to his chest until the burning settles. The bartender watches him. "Hey buddy, are you okay?"

"Yeah, I'm okay. This is the first time I ever had a drink and I didn't know it would burn." He asks for another one.

"Sure thing," the bartender answers. He pours him another one and sits it in front of him.

John is now prepared for the burn this time as he

gulps it down. After a while he starts feeling sad, and he cries as he talks to the bartender. "Jasmine says she's two months pregnant and my wife knows it. Man, I don't know what to do...this all just happened tonight. So, I came in here to get a drink and try to clear my head." And then he begins to cry harder. "You see, I love my wife, I really do. The affair just kind of happened. And I told my wife that. But you want to know what she told me? Man, she said I could have stopped it. And she's right, but I didn't. Why didn't I stop it?" He just sits there for a while just crying, then finally starts to get up. "How much do I owe you?" He pays and turns to leave but he is staggering.

The bartender says, "Hey, buddy, you're in no condition to drive. How 'bout I call you an Uber?"

But John feels that he's ok. He doesn't even realize that his speech is slurred. "I don't live that far from here. I'll be all right."

"Come on, man I'm trying to keep you safe."

"Ok," John says, and sits back down.

The Uber driver comes into the bar. "Did someone call for an Uber?" he asks the bartender. Yeah, I called you for my friend here," the bartender says. During the ride home John starts to feel a little sick, but he manages to make it home and into the bathroom before getting sick. He falls right into bed with his clothes on and falls asleep.

The next morning, John can barely open his eyes, for he has an enormous headache. Trying to move, he notices that his clothes are still on—something he never does, so it makes him wonder where he had been the night before. Looking around, he realizes that he's home, but his mind is still in a fog. He lays there trying to think, and then it all comes flooding back to him: Jasmine, baby, Sheila, and drinking at the bar.

He slowly struggles to sit up in the bed but keeps his eyes closed while he's moving. Once he has settled into a somewhat sitting position, he opens his eyes. He doesn't know why he thought that sitting up would make him feel better. His head still hurts but now he feels sick to his stomach, as well. He ignores his enormous headache and rushes to the bathroom as his mouth begins to fill with a watery substance, and he partially vomits in the toilet. He stays there until the contents of his stomach have been released, then cleans up the bathroom.

Now his stomach feels better but his head is still hurting. Not knowing what to do and not realizing that he's experiencing a hangover, he immediately thinks he needs to have a cup of coffee. He takes a shower, brushes his teeth, puts on some underwear and a t-shirt and goes into the kitchen to make a cup of coffee. He gets back into bed, feeling exhausted.

He looks at the clock and can't believe it's 9:00. He should have been at work hours ago. He looks for his cell phone, which is at a 45 percent charge, and puts it on the charger. He calls his boss and tells him that he is sick and will try to make it in tomorrow. Then it suddenly comes to him that he doesn't have his car. He remembers that he took an Uber home from the bar and his car was left on the street near the bar. He gets up to check and see if he has his car keys. He has them, but he's in no condition to pick up his car now and decides to get it later.

But now he has to deal with the embarrassment of

going to a bar in the first place, and the fact that his situation took him to another place outside of his character. John had been proud of the fact that he was a man who had never had a drink in his life, and now this. Not only did he drink, but he got drunk, but it's something that he will have to deal with later. He's glad that no one at the bar knew him. His headache is still the same after drinking his coffee, so he takes two Aleve and goes back to sleep.

It's 1:00 when he awakens again, and he's hungry now that he's emptied all the contents of his stomach. He makes himself a bacon, egg and cheese sandwich on wheat toast. He feels a little better but he still takes two more Aleve.

He gets dressed and calls an Uber to take him to get his car. About a half an hour later, the Uber driver arrives. John gets in and tells him where to go, which is about eight blocks from his place. If he had been feeling better, he might have walked it because it's a nice day.

John tells the driver to drop him off on the next block past his car, because he wants to see where his car is first. He isn't sure whether he had parked it a block before the bar or not; all he remembers is that it's near the bar. He pays the driver, gets out, and walks to his car, hoping to not be seen by anyone. He just wants to get in his car and go back home.

Once John returns, he secludes himself with the comforts of home for the rest of the day and the next day, as well. His feelings are all over the place, and he spends the time in utter disbelief as he tries to sort out everything. He is confused as to how Sheila and Jasmine really found out about each other, angry because he still feels that he had been set up, and trapped after hearing Jasmine say that she's pregnant, an announcement that nearly knocked him off his feet. *I do not know if she's telling the truth or lying,* he thinks. *I know she has been expressing and showing me that she wants more out of our relationship, but I just liked it how it was so I started backing away. Now she has been calling me several times a day, but I do not answer it. I have not been seeing her long, but things happened rather fast and I was caught up with her. I do remember her saying she was on the pill. But I could kick myself for not making sure she was still on it before I started having sex with her.*

He's thinking too much now, and the pressure of this is making his headache try to return. He realizes that he hasn't eaten, so he fixes something fast then sits on the couch, trying to relax and watch TV while he eats. But his mind keeps playing it all back, trying to comprehend everything as questions form in his head. *What am I going to do? Is Jasmine pregnant?* He sits there for a few hours until he starts to feel sleepy, then goes to bed.

It's Saturday and John wakes up feeling good and without a headache. The sun is shining and he is ready to start his day. He gets up, takes a quick shower and throws on some ball shorts and a t-shirt, for he is meeting his boys to run some ball. He hopes that that will clear his head.

Things start out okay, but he can't focus enough and his game is so off that his friends finally ask him if he's ok. "Yeah," he lies, "I guess it's not my day." He really wants to confide in them about his situation to get their opinion, because his boys are all professional men who have experienced some crazy stuff in their own lives.

One of his friends, Terry, a professional counselor, takes him aside. "You look like you have something on your mind. We can talk about it if you like."

"Nah, man I'm all right," John says, embarrassed at first. But after the game he says to Terry, "Can I holler at you for a sec before you leave?" John tells him about his situation and they head to the benches to talk.

"Oh WOW, man, that's a lot to deal with," Terry says. "You need to find out how do they know each other and then see whether she's pregnant. Then you will have to take it from there as to figuring out your next move. But let me ask you this: what are your feelings about each woman?" John tells him that he loves Sheila, his wife, but he does have strong feelings for Jasmine, the other woman.

"When did you find out all of this?" Terry asks.

"Two nights ago they both came to my apartment and waited for me to come home. They confronted me and I walked away and got in my car to leave. Sheila followed me and banged on the car door, and I let her in. And man, she cried and she even beat on me a little. I drove back home and I haven't spoken to her since."

"As a friend and professionally, I think you need to first call your wife to at least see if she is all right," Terry says. "And John, I would do that tonight...you don't want to have too many days go by."

"All right, man, I hear you," John says. "I'm going to call her tonight. And can we keep this...you know..."

"Yeah man, I know. It's cool. I'll just send you my bill." They both laugh and head for their cars.

John takes his time going home as he mulls over what to say to Sheila when he calls her tonight, turning a half an hour drive into more like an hour. Once home, he takes a long, hot shower, fixes something to eat, and heads to the living room to relax and watch a movie before he calls Sheila in a few more hours.

But his mind goes to Sheila, how he hated seeing her cry the way she did and the way they left each other two nights ago. He does want to see if she is ok, but he knows she is going to have questions that he will probably not be able to answer. He thinks about the pastor, and he wants to ask Sheila for his number to see if he can give him some spiritual advice. He finally picks up the phone and starts dialing, but quickly hangs up because he is afraid of her reaction. He calls her again a few minutes later. She answers on the third ring, just when his mouth goes dry.

"Hello?"

Clearing his throat, he says, "Hi. How are you doing?"

"I am trying not to resent and hate you. You really hurt me, John. I do not know how to handle this. Now I'm going through that 'if-only-I' thing—you know, if only I had asked Jasmine more questions, got more details. If only I had asked her what is his name. Maybe she would not be carrying your baby. How am I supposed to face her, let alone watch her grow bigger carrying your child? How can I stay professional and not turn this personal and have her fired? What am I supposed to do? What are *you* going to do?"

John sighs heavily. "Sheila, I do not have any

137

answers. I am sorry for all the pain and hurt I am causing you. I need help sorting this out and I wanted to get from you Pastor's number. Maybe you should talk to his wife to help you, as well."

"Oh, don't be trying to tell me to talk to someone because you can't solve the problem you created."

"Yeah, you're right. I am sorry...I just said it because you said you don't know how to handle it. Yeah, I did put you into this situation."

"Oh whatever, John. Do you want Pastor's number or not?"

"Yes, I do. And please, Sheila, don't be that way. I know this is hard."

"Look, right now it is hard for me to talk to you, John. You should have talked to Pastor before you started this affair. You got me here now alone trying to deal with all these emotions I'm having, and now you call me wanting to know how I'm feeling. I'm feeling hurt, I'm feeling betrayed, and I'm feeling alone. Is that enough for you? Because I can tell you some more if you want. You know what, John, forget it. I can't do this with you right now. Look, do you want this number? Are you ready? Here it is." She hangs up.

THIRTEEN

Sheila is emotionally drained as they drive back to John's apartment, and after hitting John the way she did she's now physically drained as well. She cannot believe all this is happening and she does not know why she got in the car with him. Now she's sitting there silently trying to control herself from having a breakdown in front of him, as her tears slide down her face. Her heart is completely broken. When they get to his place all she can do is get out of the car. She has no fight left, nothing in her. She is just numb. She walks to her car, gets in and pulls off. She manages her way home, where she crawls into bed, gets under the covers and cries her eyes out. She cries so hard that her throat starts to hurt and she develops a headache, but eventually falls asleep.

When she wakes the next morning, her eyes are puffy from all the crying and her head is still hurting. Her thoughts go right back to the night before; she fights back the tears, because her head hurts enough as it is. She lays there completely broken, unable to focus because her mind keeps playing everything repeatedly against her will. She has lost control of her thoughts and all she wants to do is stay in the bed and hide, closing herself off from everybody. She is embarrassed for what he is putting her through. She had been just somewhat accepting of the fact that he'd been cheating on her, but now he tops it off with this. *How irresponsible could he be? How can our marriage survive this?* She thinks. Tears begin to fall, but then something inside of her makes her get up. She decides she is not going to let him nor his actions dictate her future, she is.

She gets up feeling a little burst of energy, so she does some light cleaning around the house. She makes some lunch and is eating when her phone rings. Looking at the display, she sees it's John. For a quick second her heart leaps, and then reality comes rushing back quickly—along with her attitude—as she answers the phone. When John asks her how she's doing it gives her even more of an attitude. She honestly tells him how she feels, then gets annoyed with him telling her maybe she should go see Pastor's wife, all because he wants to see the pastor now to help him. Why didn't he think about the pastor before all this happened? She keeps their conversation short because she's too hurt to talk to him.

Sheila mopes around the house all day, trying to process everything concerning Jasmine. Right now, she hates them both and it is tearing her completely apart. So much so, that she now questions her own sanity because she swears she is losing it or has already lost it.

Then it comes to her: the realization that this nightmare does not have to be hers; she can get out. Her focus shifts from the whole situation to John. She explores her feelings for him. She realizes that beneath all her hurt and pain there is still love for him, but she also has a big hole in her heart that is filled with mistrust, fear, and doubts.

Who am I kidding? John's right, she later thinks. *I'm calling Lady Campbell.*

"Hello?"

"Hi, Lady Campbell. It's Sheila Moore."

"Oh hi, Sheila! How are you? I have missed you in church."

"I know. I am losing it…John is having a baby by my co-worker—a woman I helped to get hired."

"Your co-worker? Sheila, this is serious."

"That is why I need to see you."

"Of course! When?"

"I was hoping now, if you could."

"Yes, I will see you in half an hour."

"Thank you."

After hanging up with Sheila, Lady Campbell tells her husband what Sheila told her and that she's going to meet her at the church. "I know, I just hung up with John," Pastor says. "This is a troubling situation. I'm seeing John tomorrow. I've received about ten calls within two weeks about marital problems. I think this is a rising issue that needs to be addressed."

"Yeah, I agree. I've also been receiving disturbing calls day and night with women crying, asking for help. Some want a divorce. I tell you, the devil is busy trying to destroy marriages and God's plans."

"And you're so right, Patricia. But this thing here is a global attack. The devil is at war against marriages, especially Christian marriages, and he's trying to accomplish two things: first, he will be destroying the yoke of covering because they will no longer be praying earnestly for each other. Second, the dynamics of the family will be broken and become more dysfunctional by putting one against the other and causing children to side with one parent over the other."

"I know. Look how we were when we were just engaged. I don't want to think about what could have happened in our marriage. God showed us favor. Now let me get out of here so I can meet Sheila."

"Ok, we talk more about this later. We got to try and help our members. Maybe we can have classes and seminars."

Sheila leaves out to meet Lady Campbell in hopes that she can help her see her way through this new situation John has created. Once she gets to church, Lady Campbell greets her and they go right into prayer. "God, please meet me in my situation, mend my broken heart and bring peace to my troubled mind," Sheila prays. She also tells the devil to take his hands off her marriage.

After praying, Lady Campbell asks what happened, and Sheila explains the situation to her. "I feel like I'm on the edge of a breakdown," she says, and cries uncontrollably for about 15 minutes as Lady Campbell hugs her.

"It's ok to release it…you don't have to hold it in any longer. I know what you're feeling and you're not on the edge of a break down. You're feeling the effects of being broken. It may make you feel alone and that no one cares, and cause you to want to isolate yourself from people because you're embarrassed. Being broken also puts you in another state of mind, causing your rational thoughts to become irrational."

"But I do feel isolated," Sheila says. "I feel like everybody knows, and I'm now alone and I'm scared. I was embarrassed that he's cheating on me, but now this goes beyond embarrassment. And honestly, I want to lay down and never get up. I thought I could handle the cheating but now that he's having a baby that's another thing—a baby that we should be having." Sheila looks at Lady Campbell with tears in her eyes.

"Oh Sheila, I know how much you wanted his child and I know it hurts. You're not alone; I'm going to help you through this. But now is the time you need to turn it over to the Lord and stand on his word and trust in him. For God said in Deuteronomy 31:6, 'Be strong and of good courage, do not fear nor be afraid of them: for the Lord your God, He is the one who goes with you. He will not leave you nor forsake you.' He also said in Psalm 46:1, 'God is our refuge and strength, a very present help in trouble.'"

"But Lady Campbell, I don't know what to do."

"At this point, there's nothing you can do but let it go and let God work it out for your good. So just stretch out your faith and believe and stand on God's word to carry you through. And in time each day will get a little easier."

John has a 9:30 meeting with Pastor Campbell. He hopes he can once again bring some clarity to yet another situation he has gotten into. Right now he lies in bed, trying to sleep, but his mind is plagued with thoughts of both women in his life. He slowly falls into a deep sleep and dreams that he's at home, his real home with Sheila, and they're about to eat dinner. They're happy and having a good, romantic dinner when the doorbell rings. Sheila gets up to answer it and there's Jasmine, standing at the other side with her big stomach, and saying, "Where's John? Where my baby daddy at?" She begins to holler out his name in a state of rage.

John suddenly jumps up from his sleep in a panic, because the reality is she could very well be carrying his child. He's hot and drenched in sweat, so he pushes the covers off him. He looks at the clock and realizes that it's only 7:47 am. He tries to lie back down, but that dream has really messed him up. He can't go back to sleep, so he just lays there for a while staring at the ceiling. After about 20 minutes, he gets up, takes a shower and gets dressed. He goes into the kitchen to eat something but he has no appetite, so he just makes a cup of coffee.

John arrives at church and greets Pastor Campbell, who sees that John is tense so he goes right into prayer. Afterwards, he says, "Man, I can feel your tension when we hugged. What's gotten you so tense?"

"I was somehow set up by my wife and my mistress the other day. I parked at my apartment complex, hopped out, and started walking when I saw Sheila walking towards me and then I see Jasmine coming up behind her. I was surprised and shocked, to say the least. And then Sheila walked right up to me and slapped me, saying how could I do this to her.

Now I'm confused as to how they found out about each other and I'm feeling quite upset because I feel like I was set up. So I've got Sheila on one side crying and Jasmine on the other saying some story, that they work together and that Sheila was here just to help her confront me as her boyfriend and they had no idea that I had some type of relationship with them both. Come on now, what kind of lame story is that? And what are the odds of that being true? And then Jasmine blurts out that she's two months pregnant. *That* made me stumble backward against someone's car. When I regained my composure, I said nothing and just walked back to my car. Sheila followed me and I drove off with Sheila, leaving Jasmine standing there. I haven't been talking to her in weeks and she's been calling me several times a day…it's like she's desperate. I need some help sorting all this out."

"Well John, you really do have a serious situation here. And let's talk about your feelings of being upset."

"Yeah, I'm angry."

"At who?"

"At the both of them. They didn't have to do me like this with them both coming and attacking me together."

"Is it really them you're angry with or is it the fact that this whole thing is falling apart and you can't control it because you don't know how to deal with it, not to mention the fact that you're scared?"

There's a long pause before John answers. "I didn't plan for all this to happen in the first place. I was trying to end it with Jasmine, that's why I haven't been responding to her calls. And the truth is, she's started telling me she wants more."

"What you're saying is that you were feeling pressured by her now and so now you're running away from her too?"

"Yeah but it's not like that. I do want to see if my marriage can work, especially after our counseling. And I do love Sheila."

"So what are your feelings for Jasmine?"

"My feelings are strong for her, but I can't say that I love her."

"John, your anger is not towards them; it's at yourself. They are only victims of a deep-rooted issue of yours. You see, part of your problem is that when you feel cornered or every time you're confronted with an issue and you can't easily defuse it by fast talking or smooth your way over it, you move into tactical mode and you attempt to manipulate situation by any means necessary. You get mad and rant and rave as a plan of intimidation, and if that doesn't work you go to your last step: you shut down and eventually you escape the situation. I believe that's what's happened with you and Sheila. You were going through each step, but she was still, as we men call it, 'nagging' you, and you found an escape through Jasmine."

John just sits there, processing everything for about ten seconds before he can even respond. "You know what, no one has ever told me about myself before."

"Well, it's just that I have been a pastor for a very long time. I've learned to be good listener and pay close attention to what's said as well as to what's not being said. Now I can try to help you with counseling one on one and sessions with Sheila, but as far as Jasmine goes y'all need to have a conversation, especially if a child's involved."

Sheila wakes up feeling uneasy. She hasn't found her place in this whole situation and she's not sure how she will react when she sees Jasmine today. The weekend went too fast, and she needs more time to process everything but she can't call out.

She gets up and gets on her knees, prays, then makes the bed and goes into the bathroom. She takes a shower and gets ready for work. She thinks that if she can get to work before Jasmine does she won't have to walk in and see her. That way, she can ease her way into seeing her when she's ready. She feels good with that decision so she hurries to finish getting ready. As she's ready to leave, she goes downstairs, puts the alarm on and heads out the door.

Sheila arrives at her job feeling confident that Jasmine is not there yet. She parks her car in the parking garage, steps into the elevator, pushes the button to her floor, and just as the elevator doors open she begins to smile, expecting to see an empty reception desk. But when the doors are fully open, there sits Jasmine. Sheila she steps out of the elevator, her mouth open. She almost speaks what she's thinking: *Why are you here early? What is this? She's throwing me off and I can't let her see me off.* She quickly walks to her office, holding her breath that she wouldn't say anything—at least not yet. Well, so much for that plan.

Once in her office, Sheila closes the door. Letting out a big sigh of relief, she falls right into her chair. *Come on Sheila, girl, get yourself together,* she thinks. After she gets over the initial shock she now wonders why Jasmine really is there so early. She's never early unless she's making up some late time, but she hasn't been late recently. *What is she up to? Now I don't trust her.* And now Sheila thinks that she doesn't know her that well and tries to remember everything she can about her—that she has a daughter, and that she and the baby daddy at one point had a violent relationship before he moved to the next town. *Then she started seeing my husband. Of all the men in this world, why mine?* She was also seeing other guys during that time, one of which was married while the others had girlfriends. But Jasmine said she never knew that until she started having feelings for them. She had simply told Sheila that she just wants someone to love her and to be hers. *I don't know, it just seems strange to me with all of this going on. Is she trying to prove something or make some type of point to me?* For now, Sheila has to shake it off and try to focus on work.

Mr. Gilford has just given Sheila a new case and he calls her into his office. She's not sure why because he just handed her this case before she left the night before, but she goes to his corner office and knocks on his door.

"Come in."

"Hi, you wanted to see me?"

"Oh Sheila, come in and have a seat. This won't take long. You know we ask our clients to give us their feedback about our services, professionalism, and some other things."

"Yes."

"Well, you are our newest investigator and the response from all your clients was excellent in all areas. Their comments were that you handled their case like it was personal to you and you were sensitive to their feelings. I just wanted to congratulate you and say keep up the good work. You seem to have a knack in handling the marital cases. I'm giving you a $500 bonus."

"Oh, Mr. Gilford, thank you so much!" Sheila leaves his office, smiling and feeling happy.

She returns to her office and opens the folder of her newest client. It's another marital case, this time a husband seeking an investigation on his wife. Her mouth drops open when she sees the name Steven Carter, who wants his wife, Traci Carter, investigated. They've been married for seven years and have a five-year-old son, Steven Jr.

Sheila's hands shake so that she has to put the paper down. *Oh God, why?* she prays. *Why, out of all agencies he had to call ours and Mr. Gilford accepted his case and give it to me? Lord, what do I do? I need your help. This is my best friend's husband and her marriage is on the line.* She sits there for a while, waiting for an answer before the words "conflict of interest" come to her mind. *Yes, that's right, so I can't take this case.* She lets out a big sigh of relief. She gets up, goes back to Mr. Gilford's office, and knocks on his door.

"Come in."

Thank you, she says silently to God as she opens the door. "Can I disturb you for a few minutes?"

"Of course, Sheila. What is it?"

"It's about this case you gave me."

"What, is something wrong?"

"Yes, I have a conflict of interest here. I know this couple. In fact, the wife is my best friend. So I'm afraid I'll have to give this back to you." She places the folder on the edge of his desk.

"Ok, we'll make a trade, then. I'll try you out with

a check fraud case. I'll come over to your office with the case folder and instructs on how to go about handling this case."

"Ok. Thank you, Mr. Gilford." She walks out and goes back to her office. But her only problem now is she still knows that Steven hired someone to follow Traci.

FOURTEEN

This time when Steven swings at Paul, Paul swings back and they begin to fight right in the church's parking lot. The church is always having something going on and some people are already there.

"How dare you come here and tell me you are in love with my wife?" Steven hollers. His temper flares and he lands a solid right, hitting Paul in the face. Paul's temper is equally flared and lands a good one on Steven in return.

Traci knows better than to come in between them. "Stop it!" she yells sternly, but they continue as if she isn't there. Realizing the severity of the situation, she panics and continues to yell. "Please, stop it! Help, help…can somebody help me?" She tries to pull on Steven in an effort to get him to stop but he pushes her away. Then she goes to Paul. "Please stop," she pleads, and tries to pull on him. But he, too, pushes her away which makes Steven even angrier—first because Traci went to him and secondly, because he pushed her.

Traci sees blood. Out of desperation she screams, "Help, help me, please!" Suddenly a car pulls into the lot and she runs over to it. By the time the car parks Traci's there, reaching for the car door handle. Seeing that it's a few deacons in the car, she says, "My husband is fighting and they won't stop. Please help me!"

The deacons get out of the car and follow her. By the time they reach the fight, Paul has Steven pinned against a car but Steven is still fighting back. Both are bleeding. The deacons pull them apart. "Minister Carter, what is going on here?" Deacon Riley says.

Steven tries to look at Deacon Riley through puffy eyes, as the sun beams down on them. "We were heading into the church for counseling when someone called out to Traci and so we stopped. He comes up to us and tells me he is in love with my wife, and I swung at him."

As Steven is still talking, the police pull up and ask what happened. Deacon Riley explains everything to the officers. "We have it all under control now."

"Does anyone need any medical attention?" one of the officers asks. Paul says no, and so does Steven. "Ok…does anyone want to press charges?"

Steven says, "Yes, I do."

"Steven, no! Don't do this, please," Traci pleads.

The officer cuffs Paul, puts him in their car, and they pull off.

Deacon Riley asks them if they're ok. "Yes, thank you," Traci says, upset and shaking.

"Yeah, I'll be all right," Steven says.

Pastor Campbell walks out towards them. "What in God's name happened here?" He looks at his minister, beaten and bleeding.

Deacon Riley says, "Let me get you something so you can kind of clean up a little."

Steven tells Pastor everything and he apologizes for fighting in the church parking lot. Traci also apologizes and she feels extremely embarrassed, because now that the deacons know she feels that in no time the entire church will know, too.

Deacon Riley comes back, hands Minister Carter some paper towels, and then leaves. Pastor Campbell says, "Well, you better go home, attend to yourself, and call me later to reschedule. "

But Steven says, "If you don't mind, Pastor, I need to talk to you now."

"Ok, we can all go into the church. Steven, we can get some ice and put it in a baggie for your eye."

"Thank you, that would be good but let me go to the restroom first."

"Yes, let me go too," Traci says.

"Ok, then Lady Campbell and I will meet you both in my office."

Paul has been trying to explain his situation to the officers for about an hour now, but all they kept saying is that charges have been pressed and in order for him to be released he must pay bail or the charges be dropped. "What about my one phone call?" Paul asks.

"Come on and make your phone call," one of the officers answers.

Who am I going to call? Paul thinks. He can't call Traci, so he calls Jasmine reluctantly.

Jasmine is sitting around at home when her phone rings. When she answers, she is surprised to hear, "You have a collect call from Paul. Do you accept the charges?" She says yes.

"Hello?" Paul says.

"Paul, why are you calling me collect?"

"It is kind of a long story...I will tell you but I need your help. Can you pick me up from the Police Station in West Hill on 19th Street?"

"Police station? What! Yeah, of course."

"Oh, and can you bring $500 to bail me out?"

"Ok, I will be there soon." She rushes out to get Paul. When arriving at the police station, Jasmine pays Paul's bail, which ends up being $250, and they release him.

Paul came out and says, "Jasmine, thank you. I will pay you back."

"Ok, but what happened?"

"Let's get out of here first." They walk outside. When they got into the car he says, "I need you to take me to my car...it is in a church parking lot." Then he tells her everything.

"Wow, Paul, I did not know you were even seeing someone. I really thought that you were jealous of my relationship." She adds, "Since we are being honest here, I have something to tell you myself."

"What is it?"

"I am two months pregnant. And yes, he is married, I just found out, to my co-worker, the woman who helped me get this new job."

"Wow, it looks like we both got ourselves into situations. Did you tell him you are pregnant?"

"I did." She explained everything to him.

"So, what did he say?"

"He said nothing. He walked away to his car, his wife followed, and they drove away."

"Oh, he's a coward. What are you going to do?"

"I am not sure, but he is not getting away with this. You were somewhat bold telling that man that you are in love with his wife."

"Oh yeah, I guess I was, huh? I did not know what else to do; I did not want to lose her. Now after this she probably will not talk to me." They arrive at Paul's car four hours later from when he parked it. It was the only one in the lot. He hugs Jasmine, says thank you again, and tells her he will pay her back.

Steven and Traci knock on Pastor Campbell's door before they walk in. Before they get started, Lady Campbell opens in prayer, asking God to call up the hurt feelings and allow them to express them in a way that will be pleasing to him and brings healing. She prays for peace of mind and that God would bring healing to this broken marriage. Then she asks, "Who would like to begin?"

Steven says, "I would like to begin first by saying again that I'm sorry for my behavior. But as a man I could not just let this man walk up to me and tell me that he is in love with my wife. And I guess the fact that my wife had been with him made him feel that he had the right to tell me that he's claiming her. And so out my anger and frustration because of this situation—a situation which she caused—I reacted and punched him."

"Ok, Steven," Pastor says, "Let's talk about your anger and frustrations."

"My anger stems from that fact that my wife cheated on me."

"What did it do to you?" Lady Campbell asks.

Steven, still a little angry, says, "She hurt and betrayed me, and now, I don't trust her. I don't even sleep in the same bedroom with her anymore. I sleep in the basement in the man cave. She cheated on me, she never gave me a clue that my marriage was in trouble. She never gave me a chance to know what was wrong so I could at least try to fix it. She just gave up on me, where I never gave up on her. And that hurts, how could she just forget me like that? She looks me in my face and lies to me. And here she is now saying she stopped seeing him and talking to him. I just don't know how long it would have continued if I hadn't caught them. And now I must ask…how did he know we were going to be here today?"

Pastor says, "Ok, let Traci answer that and explain what she's been feeling."

Traci says, "I apologize too…and to answer that question, the last time I spoke to him, I told him I was going to make a counseling appointment for next week to fix my marriage."

Steven jumps in. "So are you saying you didn't tell him the day or time of our meeting, or did you?"

"No Steven, I only told him that I was making an appointment for next week."

"Ok, so if you didn't tell him how did he know we would be here?"

"I don't know…maybe he was following me. I

don't know."

"Traci, did you tell him what church you go to or not?"

"I don't know. I might have in a conversation."

Now Steven's voice is rising. "Are you kidding me? What else have you might have told him in a conversation? What does he know about us and our lives? This man can do anything and you supplied him with all our information. I don't even know if it's safe for me or my son to stay there. You jeopardized your family for him. Is that what you want, Traci? Do you want him or do you want your family?"

Traci begins to cry. "Steven, I'm sorry. I didn't mean to cause all this. I'm sorry I hurt you and I'm here because I want you and my family back. I know it's going to take time but I ask can you please try to forgive me? I'm willing to do whatever it takes to win your trust and confidence back in me and our marriage. Steven, I do love you and I know it may be hard for you to believe that now, but I do." She sits there, tears falling down her face.

Steven is moved in his heart but not in his head, so he doesn't react to Traci's emotional outburst. "I need a lot more from her than words; I want to see things by her actions and the consistency of her actions." The only thing that kind of bothers Steven is his son's thoughts and feelings about his sleeping downstairs now.

"Ok," Pastor Campbell says, "I think we made some great progress here today. And we are not going to solve or come to a solution to fixing your marriage in one session. So, here are a few things that I would like the both of you to do. I want you two to start to pray for one another, that is, if you're not already doing that. Steven, I heard you say that you want Traci to start proving herself by her actions."

"Steven, that means you will have to be more present and visible in your marriage for Traci to show you that she wants you. Are you willing to put your feelings aside to give Traci the chance to try to make things right with you and her?"

"Yes, Pastor, I hear you. I will give her the chance."

"Well ok then, I guess we can end things here and we will see you both back here in three weeks." Pastor Campbell closes out with prayer, then they all hug and exchange good nights. Steven and Traci leave the church and get into their cars, neither one of them saying a word.

Steven is still furious with her and the situation she has got him into. Now he's complicated the situation by throwing the first punch to the guy she was having an affair with and starting a fight with him in the church's parking lot. He's embarrassed beyond measure that the deacons had to be the ones that came and break them up, so all he wants to do right now is just get away from there. He can't even pick up his son, so he will have to call his mom to see if he can spend the night. Steven just pulls off, his mind going in all different directions because now he has more questions than answers.

He really wants to know how this guy found out where they attend church, and what else he knows about them. He's also not sure if Traci is telling the truth that she didn't tell him what church they go to. He even wonders whether she's really stopped seeing him and communicating with him all together. Steven still has flashes of images of Traci being with him.

Besides all of this, he doesn't really know how to handle the pain from Traci cheating on him, which has opened his old feelings and insecurities regarding her past. But what hurts him the most is that it was with someone from her past, a patron that she was all too familiar with. To Steven, it's the ultimate betrayal, because she knows how her past has affected him.

Traci steps outside, wanting to talk further with Steven. But he walks right to his car, making her feel once again like he's avoiding her. She doesn't want to cause another scene, so she just gets into her car and pulls off a few minutes after him. At first she thinks she'll just follow him home, but when he turns in a different direction she just drives home. It's a beautiful day; the sun is shining and the sky is clear, but she cannot enjoy it.

Traci has an unsure feeling, because she could sense how angry Steven was getting in their session. She wants him to know how sorry she truly is, that she really does love him, and she wants their marriage to work. But the way he acted today was no different than how he is at home. Steven didn't sugar coat anything in front of Pastor and First Lady, and neither did she.

Traci isn't sure what to expect when Steven does come home. She has a feeling that Little Steven is not coming home tonight, so she takes the time to think about everything that just happened today. She's full of emotions because she doesn't know where her marriage stands, and now she fears that Steven is reverting back to his old self: a man easily provoked into fighting because of his bad temper and overly cautious when it comes to her and other men.

Steven has come a long way from being that man,

and now she is realizing how her actions have affected him. Traci is afraid that Steven may take Little Steven and leave her. The burden of all this leads her to kneel before her couch and pray to God.

Traci racks her brain trying to remember whether she mentioned to Paul where she goes to church, but she can't come up with anything. But she does remember that he followed them to their house the time when Steven first found out about them. She wonders about how if he did that what else he could have done. Has he been following her all this time and she never realized it? Was Steven right? What does he know about them? Should they be concerned about him and their safety in their home?

She shakes her head as she tries to brush off these thoughts. She thinks Paul is not like that. He's a real nice man who just has some issues with his daughter's mother, that's all. *I don't think he's harmful. But if he did follow me to the church why would he do this? Wait a minute...* Her thoughts are interrupted with another thought. She remembers their last conversation where she had told him that she was trying to save her marriage and was going to make an appointment for them to see her pastor for counseling. She had told him that they were over and she was giving her marriage a chance. She remembered questioning his ominous response of, "You do what you feel you need to do and so will I."

"Oh my God," she says out loud, "Was this what he meant by saying 'so will I'? Oh no, he was following all this time just waiting for me to come here so he can do this. I must tell Steven, but he won't even talk to me."

Traci begins to think that he could be outside right

now. She runs upstairs and peeks out the window, looking in all different directions to see if she could spot his car. She doesn't, but she still has an uneasy feeling just knowing that he has been following her.

Trying not to panic, she goes downstairs and begins to check all the doors and the windows to make sure they're locked. Then she calls Steven's phone. "Please, pick up," she says to herself. But the phone just rings and finally goes to his voicemail. "Steven, please call me…I think he followed me to the church." She hangs up the phone.

Waiting to hear from Steven, she realizes that he's not going to respond to her. All she can do now is hope that he will return home. With the doors and windows locked, she decides to cook something to help relax her. That way, if Steven should come home dinner will already be prepared.

FIFTEEN

Paul keeps calling Traci. Wanting to hear her voice, he calls again. The phone rings once, twice, three times, and on the fourth ring he hears her and all is almost well in his universe.

Traci, seeing Paul's calls, tries to ignore them, but he keeps calling her. She finally answers just to stop him from calling her again.

"Hi, Traci. Oh baby, I miss you. Are you ok? He didn't hurt, you did he?" His words come out all in one breath.

"Paul, no, I'm fine."

"Where's he at now?"

"He's in the basement."

"Ok, good. Can you come out? I need to see you for myself. I'm here. I'm outside."

"You're what? Paul, Steven might see you!"

"Go to the window. I'm going to flash my lights at you." She rushes to the window and parts the blinds, and he flashes his lights at her. "Tell him you have to get something from the store. It's still early."

"But my son is home."

"Ok, so what's the problem? Leave him with his father. Come on, Traci. I need to see you."

"Paul, look, I can't. It's over between us. I told you

162

I'm trying to work on my marriage. Stop coming over here like this. It's not good, and besides, you're making me a little paranoid."

"I'm sorry, but if you let me see you just this one time I'll stop, I promise. I just want to see for myself that you're ok, then I promise I'll stop, trust me. Please, Traci."

Traci is quiet while she thinks it over. She goes against her better judgment and says, "Ok, but I can't be long." She goes into her son's room and tells him she's going out and she'll bring back McDonald's. "Yay!" Little Steven hollers.

She goes into the basement and tells Steven she's going to the store and that she's bringing McDonald's back. "Do you want something?" While she's talking to him he never looks at her, only says no. "Steven Jr. is in his room playing," she says before turning away and heading back upstairs.

Traci puts her coat on, opens the door and steps out. She pulls out and seconds later he's following her. She drives to a park in the next town, and after Paul parks she gets into his car. He starts asking her how things are going at home. She immediately says, "Paul, I'm not here to talk about home. You have to stop all this. I just came so you can see that I'm ok."

"Traci, you can just leave him and come live with me, you and your son." He reaches for her but she leans back and starts to say something, but notices a change in his expression. His eyes look extremely intense, causing her to feel uncomfortable and alarmed. She now wishes she had followed her mind and told him no.

"You don't know how much I miss you. It feels so good to be with you right now, even though it's only for moments. And I want you to know that I know you couldn't stop him from pressing charges against me."

"Yeah, I tried to stop him but he wouldn't listen to me."

"That's all the more reason why you should leave him."

She quickly changes the subject and says, "How did you get out?"

"I called my ex-girlfriend, my daughter's mother."

"Did that cause any problems?"

"No, I just had to tell her what happened. And that made her tell what's going on with her. It was almost like a binding moment…we both have issues with someone else's spouse."

"Paul, I have to go. I got to pick up McDonald's for dinner."

"I know, but I just don't want to let you go." He gets out to open her door. As he helps her out, he hugs her for a few seconds, then opens her car door. Traci gets in her car and pulls off. She's a little shaky and she has the feeling that he's not going to stop coming by her house.

After Traci goes upstairs to leave, Steven goes to the bottom of the basement steps, listening. When he hears the chimes over the front door, he starts upstairs and then stands on the top step waiting to hear the door close. When she closes it he goes up and peeks out the window. He watches her close her car door and pull off a few minutes later. Just as he is about to turn away from the window, he catches sight of a car that he doesn't recognize pull away. He opens the blinds to see if he can tell who it is but can only see a glimpse of a man, which gives him a suspicious feeling. Is that the guy she had been seeing? His mind is going in all sorts of directions. *How does he know where we live? Did she tell him? Is she still seeing him? Did she really to the store or is she going to meet him? Does she know that he knows where we live and that he's following her?* All this has driven him crazy. *I love her and I want to trust her but I just can't right now.*

Steven goes upstairs to the second floor to check on his son. He opens his bedroom door slowly. It looks as if Little Steven has gotten every toy out, and he's on the floor crawling around with his fire trucks. "Don't worry, I'll put out the fire!" he says. Steven watches him play for a while. Little Steven grabs his firemen who are carrying a hose and pretends that the foot of his bed is a building and the firemen are putting out the fire. He finally turns and sees Steven.

"Dad! How long were you watching me?"

Steven scoops him up and hugs him for a few minutes, not saying a word. He puts him down and gets on the floor with him, and they start playing together. Little Steven instructs his father on what to do and they play for about half an hour, just the two of them, bonding together as father and son, with Little Steven stretching his mind. Being with him brings Steven joy and briefly takes his mind off his situation. Then he says, "All right, kiddo, I'm going back in the basement. Be careful up here. If you need me come on downstairs."

"Ok, I will. And if you need me, come upstairs."

Steven laughs hard, and it's the first time he's laughed since this whole situation began. It feels good. "Ok little man, you got me." He leaves the room. As he walks downstairs he peeks out the window again to check and see if Traci is coming. He heads back into the basement and checks the time. He grabs his cell phone to call her but puts it back. He wants to see how long it's going to take her. It's already been 25 minutes.

Traci quickly stops at Dress Barn and buys a suit to wear to church. Then she goes to McDonald's and now she's heading home. She really didn't need a suit, but she really does like it and besides, she couldn't come home empty-handed. Steven wouldn't believe that she went to the store and then he wouldn't trust her the next time she goes out. *This way,* she thinks, *I won't have to explain anything. He'll see from the bag even though he's probably not going to talk to me. I know he's going to be looking so I'll leave the bag in the room where I know he's going to see it, and he might look in my closet to see what I bought.*

Traci gets out of the car, grabs the bags, and opens the door. She takes a deep breath before walking in. She hollers out to Steven Jr. and walks into the kitchen to put the bags down. She checks the clock and realizes that she's been out for about an hour and a half, then goes to the basement steps and hollers out to Big Steven. "I'm home!" He doesn't answer, so she goes upstairs and opens Little Steven's door.

"Mommy, you home!"

"Yes. Where's your father?"

"He's in the basement."

"Oh, ok. Come on down to eat McDonald's."

"Yay!"

"While I'm taking your food out of the bag go tell your dad I'm home." Little Steven comes back up from the basement and says, "He knows, you told him."

"Ok, come sit down and eat." As they're eating she thinks, *Really? You're just going to ignore me now? I don't know if he'll go to counseling now.* She tries to stop thinking about it so she asks Little Steven about how he played while she was gone.

"I played that there was a fire and I had to help get someone out of the building, and Daddy was helping me."

"Oh, pretend or for real?"

"No, for real. Daddy was watching me play and then he just picked me up and hugged me. He hugged me kind of hard too, then he started playing with me. And then he told me he was going in the basement and if I needed him to come down there and I told him if he needed me to come upstairs. And Daddy laughed real hard. Mommy, why does Daddy stay in the basement?"

"Oh baby, I don't know. You have to ask Daddy why."

"Ok, I'll ask him."

After eating she tells him he can go up and finishing playing while she cleans up, then she heads downstairs. Steven is just sitting there watching TV. He doesn't turn to acknowledge her presence, so she stands in front of the TV and says, "I'm calling Pastor Campbell to set up a session and I'll let you know when it is." She turns and goes back upstairs without waiting for a response.

She checks on Little Steven to see if he wants to watch TV, then she goes in her room to take a long, hot shower. She gets out and puts on her pajamas, then tells Little Steven to start cleaning and she'll be back a little bit to check to make sure all his things are put away. "And I'll start your water for your bath. Don't just play in there but wash up, because I will check before you get out."

Traci and Steven go back to see Pastor and Lady Campbell today. It has been three weeks since their last appointment. And like before, Steven takes their son to his mother's first and will meet Traci at the church.

This time, Traci is there waiting on Steven. But she doesn't know that Steven has been there, parked across the street on the corner looking to see if this guy has followed her there again. He waits for 25 minutes before he pulls out and heads into the church's parking lot. They both get out of their cars. Traci gets out feeling uneasy, while Steven feels nonchalant.

They go into the church, where Pastor and Lady Campbell are waiting for them. Pastor prays and they get right into it. Pastor asks Steven if he wants to start off today. "Yes Pastor, I'm still struggling with the fact that Traci has cheated on me. And I still don't trust her. I'm sleeping downstairs because it's easier to avoid her. And to be honest, I don't have anything to say to her. This came out of nowhere. I didn't know that she was unhappy, she never complained or nagged about anything."

"Ok. I understand everything you just said, but you haven't told me your expectations. You know why you're here."

"Oh, well, I guess I want to know if this marriage can survive and can I ever trust her again."

"Yes, your marriage can survive and you can one

day trust her again. But it's going to take time and commitment on both parts, and it's something you both have to want. No, it's not going to be easy and it can't happen until there's forgiveness. You both will have to forgive each other. And let me tell you why: this affair did not just happen suddenly. It's a buildup of frustration, loneliness, lack of communication, unhappiness, discontent, and so forth."

"But Pastor, she never said anything; there were no warning signs until about a month ago when she told me that everything changed when I became a minister and she said she feels neglected."

Lady Campbell jumps in and says, "But you can't hold her responsible for your actions. Traci, how did things change?"

"Everything happened so fast after he answered the call from God to become a minister who visits the sick. It was like I lost him and he became committed to someone else, and now I'm just his child's mother. I'm not his wife anymore. I thought I was dealing with everything but I guess I was suppressing my feelings of no longer being wanted and feeling neglected. I didn't say anything because it's God, and what can I say? I just want him to at least balance things out."

"Ok, I understand where you're coming from Pastor says, "and this is common. When one is in the ministry and the other isn't it can cause an imbalance in the marriage, and what we have here is a somewhat normal result. Now my question to the both of you is, how you feel about each other?"

Traci says, "I love him but it's hard to love someone who doesn't talk to you and acts like you're not there."

"I just don't trust her, but I still love her. Because of my past it's hard to let things go. I'm still very angry and I'm trying not to go back to the old me. What gets me is this guy was one of her patrons when she was a dancer, and she knows how I feel about that."

Lady Campbell says, "Traci and I had a talk and she knows how much her past affects you, and she fears because of this you'll go back to your old ways before you started going to church. But I want to ask you: What do you need from her that may help you to maintain who you are now as well as help you to try to trust her again?"

"I really don't know, because when I think of her I think of her being with him and I can't get past it. I know how guys like him think, and that street side of me wants to come out and get him for taking what's mine. But on the other hand, if she's mine, how could she do this knowing how I feel about this? How could she?"

"But Steven, I admit that I was wrong for not expressing my feelings to you, and Lady Campbell helped me to see that he was just filling my void of neglect," Traci says. "I hope you can truly forgive me. But if not, I'll have to understand."

"What do you mean you understand, Traci? You caused this."

"I know, that's exactly why I said I'll understand."

"Ok now, there's no need to be placing blame— you're both guilty," Pastor says. "But Steven, you really need to focus on the good things in your marriage and consider what it's worth to you. I really want you both to evaluate things before you make any decisions either way. And I want you both to remember this: Traci, when a man selects a woman to marry him, it means that he has already opened his heart to receive her. He has already seen what type of character she has. He's seen her morals and standards, her beliefs, and they talked about her dreams. He was able to see how well they communicate together and he had some time to see if she's the jealous type. He was also able to see her personality and whether they were compatible emotionally, spiritually, intellectually, financially and physically—and yes, in that order. He also has to know that you'll fit into his world, his family, friends, his life. And after considering all these things, he decides that she is the woman that he could see himself with for the rest of his life. A woman that he can trust his heart with. She's the woman he wants to grow old with. Then he takes the risk of being rejected and offers himself to her to be her husband through the thick and the thin. And Steven, the woman has the choice to accept or reject your proposal, but you better believe she has already gone through her own process in considering if you're the right man for her. She looks at how he communicates his feelings to her, and she watches to see whether he has a temper and if he's the jealous type. She asks him questions like: How are you with money? Do you pay your bills on time? How do you treat your mother and do you get along with your family? How do you handle conflicts? She also looks at whether you're a man with dreams and a plan for his future. She will have to see if her life can co-exist with his, has he made room for her in his future and whether she can follow his lead. So, I said all that to say this, is was a process you both went through before you got married. And being married is another process that you agreed to take on and become one unit, and work together in the process emotionally, spiritually, intellectually, financially, and physically to continue your journey with this person for the rest of your life. You are also saying you're committing yourself 100 percent to that person. And no matter what comes into your lives, you are willing to face it together."

SIXTEEN

Jasmine wants to follow them and bang on the door too, but after she told John that she's two months pregnant everything else seemed to happen so fast. John walked away and Sheila followed, and the next thing Jasmine knows she's standing there crying in John's apartment parking lot, all alone, at night. It's almost winter so it's gotten dark early, with only the street lamp lighting up the lot.

Devastated and still crying, she slowly turns and makes her way back to her car, then she gets in and sits there. She's hurt and mad, and she hollers out angrily. "God, why have you allowed him to be my co-worker's husband, why? I honestly thought he was different and I knew he could be the one for me, he could be mine. But now I have to worry and hope whether Sheila will be able to forgive me and not have me fired. If only I didn't ask for Sheila's help none of this would have been happening now." She looks up and says, "God, you sure have a funny way of bringing things into the light." She starts her car up and pulls off, wondering where John and Sheila went and what they're doing. The reality of her newfound situation begins to sink in—the fact that she is two months pregnant and the baby's father just walked away, not even saying a word. She's hurt because he has already stopped communicating while all this time she's been trying to talk to him. After all this, she finds out that he's her co-worker's husband, the man that they both love and have talked about to each other.

Reality again greets Jasmine as she wakes up the next morning. She's thankful it's Saturday because she cannot face Sheila just yet. Getting up, she realizes it's after 10 o'clock. She knows her mom will be calling soon, because she took Jacqueline for the night and Jasmine told her she would pick her up first thing in the morning. But now she just cannot; she needs some time to process everything and figure out how she is going to tell her mom.

Moving slowly this morning, she takes a long, hot shower, trying to wash away her reality. But it is still there, facing her head-on: she's pregnant, with a married baby daddy who happens to be her co-worker's husband. She thinks things could not get any worse.

As she gets dressed her phone rings, but she ignores it and continues to get dress. She just sits there on the bed, consumed in her thoughts and feeling overwhelmed. She starts crying all over again and says aloud, "I need to get it together. John is not getting away with this, that is for sure."

Her phone rings again and this time she answers it. "Hey Mom."

Erika says, "Hey, are you on your way?"

"Huh? No, I'm kind of moving real slow today."

"What's going on? What is wrong with you?"

Jasmine sighs deeply. "There's something I must tell you, but I do not know how."

"Whatever it is, baby, you can tell me. I am here for you."

"Ok, mom. I'm pregnant."

Silence fills her ears before her mother says, "Well, we'll just have to deal with it. It's going to be ok."

"Mom, but that's not all. The father is my co-worker's husband."

"What! You're seeing your co-worker's husband? Oh, Jasmine, you know better than that!"

"No Mom, it's not like that. When he told me he was married, I already had feelings for him and I was already seeing him before I got this job. I had no idea he was my co-worker's husband."

"When and how did you find all this out?"

"Well, I found out the other day that I am two months pregnant and my boyfriend has not been speaking to me. So my co-worker, who is an investigator, said she would go with me to stake him out and confront him. For some reason, I never mentioned his name and she never asked. I told her how we met and that I love him. She even told me some things about her marriage. We both cried together about our relationships. Last night is when we both discovered that her husband is my boyfriend."

Erika feels the pain of not telling Jasmine's father about her. "Did you at least tell him you're pregnant?"

"Yes."

"What did he say?"

Jasmine starts crying. "Oh mom, he didn't say

anything. He just walked away, and his wife was right behind him. He got in his car, she banged on the window, he let her in, and they drove off. They drove off, Mom, leaving me standing there alone." That gives Erika a flashback to a page in her own life when she was once left brokenhearted by Jasmine's father. She, too, had watched him drive away with his fiancé, leaving her standing alone in her driveway.

Erika says, "Now we will just have to work through all of this. What do you want to do?"

"I do not know exactly, but I just cannot let him get away. He is going to be a father to our baby one way or another."

John finally calls Jasmine, even though he's still not sure what he's going to say. He figures he'll play off her reactions, so he calls her.

Jasmine looks at her phone. *Oh, I bet Sheila made him call me,* she thinks, and she answers it. "Hello?"

"Hi Jasmine, it's John. How are you?"

"I'm pregnant, John, that's how I am."

"Yeah, you shocked me with that, and I'm sorry I walked away and left you. I didn't know how to react to that because before we began being intimate you said that you was on the pill."

"Yeah John, I said I *was* and you never asked me to get back on it. So I thought you was just going to use a condom and when you didn't I thought you was ok with taking a risk."

"No, I wasn't. Jasmine, you don't get it. I don't want kids." He wants to say, *I'm not sure how I feel about the one you already have.*

Now with an attitude, she says, "Ok, well, I'm having yours and I told you this a month ago. Now

I'm three months pregnant and you're just now talking to me. Look, I want to know what you're going to do. Are you going to be in our lives or what?"

"All this is happening way too fast for me. And I'm still not sure that you're pregnant. Ok, you want me to move in with you and I will not be pressured into anything?"

"So, does that mean we still have a chance?"

"Jasmine, I don't want to mislead you. But right now I'm still trying to digest everything. So are you really pregnant and is it mine?"

"Yes, John. What type of woman do you think I am?"

"Sorry. I just had to ask."

"Ok, since you don't believe me, come to my next doctor's appointment."

"When and where is it?"

"It's in two days and it's at County Memorial Hospital on the third floor at 4 o'clock."

"Ok. I'll go to only this one appointment." They hang up.

Jasmine is putting in place a plan of action against John. She will do whatever it takes, even if it should affect her relationship with Sheila, because he will not leave her to raise his child alone.

First, she goes to his apartment complex and waits for someone to go in the building. After waiting almost an hour, she finally sees someone pull up. After they get out of their car she slowly gets out of hers and follows them inside. While they wait for the elevator, Jasmine pretends to be searching for something in her bag and pretends to have found it just when the elevator bell rings. She begins to walk toward the rows of mailboxes. She looks up his name so she can get his apartment number, and there it is: 305A. Now she goes back to her car, pulls out a pen, and writes his full address on a non-return address envelope that's already been stamped. When she gets her first ultrasound she will send him a picture of their baby. Second, if he still doesn't come around the she'll take him to court for child support, but she hopes it won't have to come to that point.

After getting John's address Jasmine goes home and calls her mom, who's been supportive and suggestive in ways to encourage her in how she should make her plan. "Hello?"

"Hi Mom, thanks for keeping Jacqueline. I'll get her some time tomorrow. It won't be late, because I'll have to get her ready for school. But I've called to tell you what I have planned. I went over to John's apartment and waited for almost an hour for someone to come home so I could get inside and look for his apartment number on the mailboxes. That's the first part of my plan. I wrote out a non-return address envelope addressed to him with a stamp already on it to mail to him when I get my first ultrasound. The second part will be to take him to court for child support if it comes to that point."

"That sounds like a good plan. Shock him into reality and then get him for support. Serves him right," her mother says. "These men think they can treat us any old kind of way and get away with it." Having flashbacks of what she went through herself, Erika continues. "They leave us alone to raise their child while we struggle to make ends meet and they go on having no cares in the world, with their freedom to do what they want. So, I'm proud of you, Jasmine, for standing up for yourself and not allowing another man to go free from his responsibilities."

"Yeah Mom, it does feel good to take charge, be in control of my own life, and not allow someone to dictate things for me."

"Just think things out first and be careful."

"I will. I'm gonna do what's best for me and my child. John and I are finally at a good place and things are working out good, but there's one thing that concerns me."

"What is that?"

"His wife."

"Let me tell you something. I know this is not about his wife, but sometimes in situations like this, no matter how hurt and upset she is with him more than likely she'll end up on his side and against you, because you're now considered to her as the other woman, you're the mistress. And you're the one that's destroying her marriage. And even more now so that you're pregnant with his child—the child she may have wished to be carrying. So keep your guard up, and at the same time try to remain close to her. Now, I know it sounds odd and it's going to be different, but she's not going to come out and tell you things now."

"Ok Mom, but this is still going to be hard for me. And it's going to be quite awkward, to say the least."

"Of course it will be, but in time it will get easier. You have to remember, she's having the same feelings you're having, but for her it's twice as hard. So, you may feel some little attacks from her. Don't worry about it, she's just trying to put a little pressure on you because she's struggling to deal with this herself."

"Ok. I'll learn to make the best of this situation and make it work."

Jasmine sits at the front desk, pleased with herself. She wants to take her stand and show Sheila her position by getting to work first, letting her know that she's not going anywhere, that she'll be right here before Sheila takes her own position and makes a stand. *I really don't want to continue to hurt Sheila, but if she gets in my way I'll do what I'll have to do,* she thinks. But the look on her face as Sheila gets off the elevator and sees Jasmine is priceless, truly a picture worth having. Her mouth drops, and she's rendered speechless and stunned. All she can do is quickly retreat to her office.

Now I believe my position was made clear to Sheila. Now I can turn my attention to John, Jasmine thinks. *First, I'll follow him around a little and see if he leads me to Sheila's house. I came to work prepared.* She had brought extra stuff for a stakeout, so after work she goes right to John's apartment complex and waits for him to come home.

She parks out of the way so he doesn't see her but where she could see him. About 30 minutes later, he pulls in, finds a parking spot and goes to his apartment. She knows his apartment number and she thinks it's facing the parking lot. She waits to see the lights come on and *bang*, there it is now—she knows which apartment is his. She gets out of the car, goes over to John's and writes down his license plate number. She gets back in her car to wait and see if he comes back out. About another 30 minutes later, his apartment lights go out and few more minutes later he comes out of the building and gets into his car. Jasmine follows him as he drives into the next township, where he turns left on Pike Street, then a right onto Cherry Oak Drive before turning into a driveway of a home and parking beside another car.

She quickly pulls over at the corner and turns off her head lights. John is out of the car and ringing the doorbell. She leans forward in her seat to make sure she gets a clear view of the door. It opens, and look who it is: Sheila. *Well, that was easy...I don't have to stake him out again,* Jasmine thinks. She grabs her pad and pen, then quickly goes over to Sheila's car and writes down her plate number and the house's address before getting back into her car and pulling off. "In one hour's time I got everything I need," she says aloud, and heads to her mom's.

Jacqueline is playing when she sees the flash of car lights outside the window. "I think my mom's here," she says to her grandmother, "Can I open the door?"

"No, if it's her she'll open it with her key."

"But I wanted to open it for her."

"Don't you bother that door, Jacqueline."

"Ok. Can I look out the window, then, to wave at her?"

"No, you wait until she gets in and then you run up to her and give her a great big hug."

"Yeah, Mommy likes my hugs."

The door opens and Jasmine comes in. Jacqueline runs to her and gives her a big hug. "Yay, Mommy's home!" Jasmine is taken aback. She drops her bag, picks her up and hugs her tightly. "Thank you!"

"For what, Mommy?"

"For your wonderful hugs."

"Oh, you welcome!" Jasmine puts her down, and Jacqueline returns to playing.

Jasmine walks over to where her mom is sitting on the couch, where she hugs and kisses her. "Mom, I wish you were there to see the look on Sheila's face when she got off the elevator this morning and saw me at my desk. Your advice worked. It was priceless, Mom. It stopped her in her tracks and she stood there with her mouth open in shock. And I didn't see much of her all day. And after work I went to John's apartment like you planned."

"So I'm at John's place, and he pulls in and goes to his apartment, which I now know faces the parking lot. After a while he comes back out, and I follow him. He goes right to Sheila's house. I also wrote down her address and license plate number too, just in case I need to leave her another little message."

"You've accomplished a lot in one day."

"Yes, Mom, I did."

"Well that's good. Just stay on your toes and watch her."

"I was thinking you should turn the heat up a little and do your second plan, send him a letter. Tell him if he doesn't step up on his own he'll be forced to by the courts by way of child support. I could even type it up for you. You'll just have to get the envelope and mail it. I'll have it ready for you tomorrow when you pick up Jacqueline."

"Mom just stop it, will you please? Let me handle John when I'm ready."

"I was just trying to help you so you won't be stressing yourself out."

"I appreciate it but let me decide what I want to

do."

"Well, I can still type the letter just in case you change your mind."

"No, Mom, I won't need it. You'll see."

"Ok. I know, stop. I'm sorry, but it's almost over anyway."

"What is almost over? What are you talking about?"

"Just trust me, Jasmine…you will know everything soon."

Jasmine is frustrated at this point and all she wants to do is leave. She tells Jacqueline to hurry and clean up so they can leave. It's times like this is when Jasmine hates that she has to leave Jacqueline with her mom. She fears that she will try to somehow use and manipulate her, as well.

On the way home, she tries to figure out what's making her mom act the way she is. Once again, she thinks it has something to do with her father—a man she knows nothing about. She has also never seen a man in her mom's life. Whenever she had asked her mom anything about her father, she would get angry and upset. Jasmine finally just stopped asking because she knows she's not going to get an answer. She can't even tell her how she feels about not having a father, let alone tell her how at times she resents her for keeping him away from her.

Jasmine has had a long day, and is about to go to bed when she catches a glimpse of herself in the mirror. *I can't believe that I'm having another child and I'm not married,* she thinks as she rubs her stomach. *I really thought things would be different with John. I just did not know he was married at the beginning. I was not planning to have his baby but I did dream of us being married and one day having a family. Now look, he will not even see me, let alone talk to me. I hate to admit it but my mom was right. I guess I do need to step things up a bit and send him a letter threating to take him to court if he doesn't help me with our son, because it will not be too long before he arrives. I need to have everything ready before that happens.* She gets into bed and calls her mom.

"Hello?"

"Hey Mom, I thought about the letter. You can go ahead and do it and have it ready for me when I pick up Jacqueline, and I'll mail it off tomorrow."

SEVENTEEN

Today Jasmine meets John at her doctor's appointment. She's not satisfied with their last conversation. It seems to her that he's trying to get out of their relationship, but he won't get out so easy.

Jasmine is sitting in the waiting room when John walks in, looking a little uneasy as he looks around at the other pregnant women and a few men that are there. He sits next to Jasmine. They wait together awkwardly, silently watching the others until her name is called and they go in the back.

The doctor comes in and mistakenly says, "This must be the happy father! So let's see the baby." She pours the cold gel on her stomach that seem to be a little bigger.

All John keeps thinking is, *If this was Sheila I would be happy.* Then he hears a sound that brings him back. "That's a strong heart beat," the doctor says. She moves the device around on Jasmine's stomach and points out the baby's features. "Let's try to see if we can tell what you're having. Well, let's hope the legs are not crossed. And look, you're having a boy!"

Jasmine turns to look at John, because she wants

to see his expression. As he stares at the screen and he looks shocked and yet amazed that it's in 3D, and that everything the baby is doing could be seen so clearly. Jasmine thinks she even sees a little excitement in John's face.

John is completely taken back as to what he's actually seeing. *Wow*, he thinks, *I can see everything…it's like he's floating around in her stomach. Oh look, he's got his finger in his mouth. This is amazing.* Now John is really having mixed feelings, but he's trying not to let it show.

The doctor's tells Jasmine everything looks good so far and asks if she has any questions. John asks, "How far along is she?" The doctor pulls Jasmine's information up on the computer. "Well, according to her last exam she was two months. She's a little over 18 weeks, which means she's a little over four months. In three more weeks, she'll be five months. Any more questions?"

"No," John says.

As they leave out, Jasmine says, "I forgot something."

"Ok, I'll talk to you later," John says.

Jasmine goes back in and asks for a few ultrasound pictures. The girl says, "Sure, come on back. I can do that for you."

John cannot explain or help the way he felt when he heard the baby's heartbeat, and especially seeing the baby so clearly in her stomach. He hadn't been expecting that or his feelings.

Sheila calls and wants John to come over to talk. He goes over, even though he really doesn't want to see her right now because he's uncomfortable with what he's feeling. Plus now, even more so he hates the fact that he even mentioned to Sheila that he was going to Jasmine's doctor's appointment.

Sheila lets him in and of course, he goes right to his spot on the couch. After sitting down herself, Sheila says, "I have called you over because I've kind of been having some second thoughts about Jasmine."

"What kind of second thoughts?"

"I don't know. It's hard to explain, but the other day I briefly spoke to her. I just asked her how she's feeling and after she responded I felt the urge to say more."

"More like what?"

"I don't know, but I just stood there and then I walked away. I know she could tell I wanted to say something."

"But what were you going to say?"

"I think I was feeling a little compassionate towards her, and I guess I let my guard down. She seems a little different to me."

"Well, Sheila, she *is* pregnant."

"No thanks to you."

John cringes at her words, knowing that he put his foot in his mouth with that comment. "Sorry, I was just saying maybe it's her pregnancy that's making her different."

"I know what you are saying but I'm not sure that she has an agenda now. I am kind of thinking she was just reacting to this new situation. And because I got her this job she might have been trying to show me that she needs this job despite the awkward situation. I don't know, but I'm still going to look and see what I can dig up. And even though I feel this way a little part of me says don't trust her."

"So what, you're going to stake her out?"

"Yeah, and other things. I'm gonna look into her background."

"And don't forget, I pretty much have access to everything in her entire life."

"Oh, I also wanted to know what happened when you went to her doctor's appointment."

"Sheila, don't do this."

"Just tell me John, how was it for you?"

"It was ok. So can we leave it alone?"

"Did you know she's showing now and she's not sick like she was?"

"No, I haven't spoken to her since her appointment."

"Why not?"

"Look Sheila, I don't want to talk about her."

"And why not? John, it's because of her our marriage broke up. You wanted her."

"Ok, Sheila, I'm not going to talk about her and I don't want to argue with you."

"I'm not arguing with you, John. I'm just asking you a question."

"Ok, well just stop with the questions. I'm about to leave anyway." He gets up and starts to walk towards the door.

"John, it's just."

"I know…that's why I'm leaving." But he's really leaving because he doesn't want to say too much about the baby, especially since she might pick up on his feelings. He says good night and leaves.

Jasmine is now five months pregnant, and she's showing. She has not seen or heard from John since her last doctor's appointment a month ago.

She lays in bed, feeling her stomach as the baby moves. She thinks, *I do not understand why he has not called me yet. I know he was excited because I saw his expression when he heard the baby's heartbeat, and he said it was amazing as he looked at the 3D image of our child. He wanted proof so now he has it and I still have not heard from him. Perhaps I did not make myself clear to him. I need to send him a message, a forget me not message.* She gets up, takes the envelope she addressed to him and puts one of the 3D pictures she got from the doctor's office in it. Then she takes a 3x5 index card and writes on it, "Forget me not, Daddy," and seals the envelope. *This should get his attention,* she thinks. And the next day she mails it along with the letter her mom has written, threatening him to go to court for child support.

John has not seen nor heard from Sheila in about two weeks. The last time he saw her, she'd given him the feeling that she was reconsidering things regarding Jasmine. John isn't sure if he should be happy and thinks that maybe they will all get along. He's also cautious because he knows how much she doesn't trust Jasmine. She even told him to watch out for her.

But now he has to talk to her about Jasmine. He wants Sheila's opinion, but he is not sure what he'll get from her because she'd been acting so unstable the last time. Still, he needs to talk to her. "Hey Sheila, how you doing? Did I disturb you? I wanted to talk to you about something."

"Well, I don't know."

"Should I tell you over the phone or should I see you?"

"How about you tell me what or who it's about,

and maybe that can determine it."

"Ok, it's about Jasmine."

"I thought you would say that. I was sort of hoping you would say it was about us…then I would have said come over."

"Oh, I wish it were about us."

"What, do you really?"

"Yeah. Because of what Jasmine is doing now, I'd rather deal with us than her."

"Deal with us? What is that supposed to mean, John?"

"Nothing, Sheila. What is wrong with you? Why are you acting funny?"

"What's so funny about me wanting us and missing you lying beside me, holding me, and kissing me? Tell me, John, what is so funny about that?"

"Nothing, Sheila."

"On the other hand, how about wanting to have your child? Is that funny too?"

"No, Sheila. Just stop this."

"No John, what's funny is you calling me about Jasmine. Yeah, that's funny. She caused all this and you want to talk to me about your mistress because you can't handle her."

"Sheila, I'm coming over."

John is at Sheila's in less than 20 minutes. He bangs on her door and she finally opens it as if she hadn't been expecting him. He walks in, looks around, and then looks at her. "Are you ok?"

"John, one day I'm good, the next day I'm not. I'm just questionable."

"What does that mean?"

"It means my stability is wavering."

"Why, what is wrong with you?"

"You are having an affair with my receptionist, and now she is having your baby. It's torture to watch her pregnant." Her eyes fill with tears.

He moves toward her and holds her close in his arms as she cries. When her crying subsides, he lifts her head, wipes her tears, and kisses her. A gentle kiss turns into a passionate moment. As John fills with desire for Sheila, he lifts her up and carries her to the bedroom, where they quickly undress and John takes her, savoring every inch of her body. Sheila is exploring him, as well. She whispers in his ear, "Please make me pregnant too," just as he explodes inside of her. He collapses on top of her and then rolls over. They lay there in silence, both lost to their own thoughts.

John is thinking he does still love Sheila, but Jasmine's baby has taken him by surprise and he's afraid of the feelings it's causing him to have. He kind of wishes Sheila was the one carrying his baby.

Sheila, laying there caught up in her emotions, is wishing the night could last forever and praying that he's gotten her pregnant too. She knows that would complicate an already complicated situation, but she can't think any further than what she feels now. She loves him and wants him to come home, but she's afraid to speak her true feelings for fear of being rejected. She doesn't know how he really feels about Jasmine and their baby.

They lay there silently until John speaks. "Look Sheila, if I could change everything I would. You must believe me, I did not plan for any of this to happen. You are the last person I wanted to hurt like this, and I am sorry."

"I'm sorry too, John. Many things have happened,

but my love for you is still there and that's why it is so hard for me to watch Jasmine carrying your child when you knew how desperately I wanted to have your child. And what makes it crazy is I still do."

John takes a deep breath. "I still love you too, Sheila. And I'm sorry for what we just did. I don't want to complicate things. But you were crying and one thing lead to another."

"Well John, I am not sorry. I have to admit I wanted you the last time you were here. I want you back home. I just don't know how you feel about Jasmine and this baby."

"Honestly, Sheila, this baby has unexpectedly changed things."

"What are you saying? How has it changed things?"

"My perception has not changed; my fears have only become more real, and yet I am excited. But my problem is somehow, Jasmine has managed to get my address. She sent me a 3D picture of the ultrasound with a note saying, 'Forget me not, Daddy.' And I cannot stop looking at it. I haven't spoken to her nor seen her since I met her at the doctor's office. She also sent me a letter saying that she's going to take me to court for child support."

"Ok John, I am putting my feelings aside and let's have a real talk. What are your feelings for her?"

"I do have feelings for her but I do not love her. And like I just said, this baby has gotten me excited but I am afraid to let my feelings show because I do not want to hurt you and because I know how you feel about Jasmine. And as far as Jasmine goes, honestly, if she knew how this baby is affecting me she'll have me see her every day. But I am not sure if

I want to take it where she wants to take it to."

"So how do you know where she wants to take it?"

"She's told me and showed me that she wants to build a future with me."

"Why are you not sure?"

"For one thing, she already has a kid, which means I would have to deal with the father and his issues. For me, it's enough just thinking about being a father myself. In addition, having a ready-made family sounds complicated to an already complicated situation."

"I hear what you're saying, but you do have to talk to her now, especially after this letter. You don't know if this is just a threat or whether she's actually filed. You have to find that out."

"I know and I'm gonna call her tomorrow."

Sheila opens the door and John walks into their house. He sits in the same spot where she last confronted him. But tonight, she's called him over to tell him what she thinks his mistress is trying to do. "I didn't tell you this before because I was trying to sort things out, but I went to work early the other day just to avoid her because I haven't figured out my position in all this," she says, "and I step off the elevator and there she is. Now there's no reason for her to be there early. She's not making up any late time. So why is she here so early? I keep on asking myself. And then I thought about how she looked—her expression was satisfied, and she had a little smirk on her face when she saw my dropped mouth and my shocked look. I hurried to my office. Later it came to me she's trying to send me a message."

"A what?"

"A message?"

"That don't make sense."

"Ok, look at the facts. She knows I'm hurt and mad at you. She knows I'll probably look at her now as your mistress. And she also knows that I will have to take a position, whether I want to or not, and it won't be with her. So I believe her message is that 'I'm here and I'm ready for whatever position you take.'"

"So, what position do you take?"

"She's right. I don't want to, but she's the one that brought all this havoc into my life. I'm with you."

"Sheila, I'm sorry for all of this."

"Yeah, John."

"No, I mean it. I didn't know you worked with her and now you have to face my mess."

"Whatever. John. Look, what are you going to do about her?"

"I'll call her and handle this."

Sheila says, "Ok, but in the meantime she sent this message for a reason—she's up to something. And we have to be ready for whatever she's going to do."

"What do you mean, whatever she's going to do?"

"I told you, she's ready and she's letting me know that she's not going nowhere."

"Ok, Sheila. I'll call her tomorrow."

"Ok, but when you talk to her say what you need to say but don't get her suspicious."

"Ok. Well, it's getting late and I better go. I'll let you know how it goes."

Sheila's feelings are all over the place. One minute she wants John back and the next she hates him for causing all this pain in her life. But tonight, she wants him there with her. She's tired of feeling lonely, let along being alone. On the other hand, this whole pregnancy thing with Jasmine has gotten to her a little more than she expected. She's trying to compartmentalize her feelings but it's hard to separate things. Whenever she thinks of John, the thought of Jasmine comes to her mind. And when she sees Jasmine at work she can't help but think of her carrying John's baby, how their lives are all now intertwined, and there is no getting around it. She's the third wheel, even though she's his wife and the other woman is his mistress. This baby has bonded them all together, which is the part that Sheila is finding most difficult to deal with, along with the fact that she has to watch Jasmine carry her husband's baby. It's something she wants to do without but can't unless she gets Jasmine fired, but she hasn't done anything wrong to be fired for. Sheila knows she'll just have to deal with it.

Sheila is realizing that the office fraud case is not as easy as she thought it was going to be. She had thought that it might be just one person stealing, but this is well organized and carefully done. She needs some advice from Mr. Gilford, so she goes to his office. He's not there, so she starts to go back to her office but instead goes to Jasmine to see if he's coming back today.

"He told me he might come back but it didn't sound definite."

"Oh, ok."

"Can I help you with something?"

"I'm just trying to get a handle on this office theft/fraud case."

"I think it's probably more than one person, and it depends on what's being taken and its size. You know someone has to be the look person," Jasmine says.

"Yeah well, the owner thought he had someone he could trust to feed him some information but that's not working out. I'll have to get inside and I wanted Mr. Gilford's advice."

"Well if he should call in do you want me to tell him to call you?"

"No, I'll try to figure it out and if I can't I'll see him tomorrow. But thanks."

"You're welcome. You know what, this feels like old times."

"Yeah, I guess it does."

"Sheila I'm sorry. I have nothing against you at all, but it's John who I have an issue with. I hope you and I can somehow patch up our friendship...we were getting close."

"We were close, Jasmine, but I don't know if we can be like we were. Jasmine, you're having my husband's baby and that's hard to get over. It probably wouldn't hurt this bad if it wasn't with you of all people. You know how badly I wanted to have his child. So it hurts to watch you get bigger."

"Oh Sheila, I know, and I am not trying to flaunt myself in front of you either. You and I are the only two women here and it's nice to talk with you. There has to be some way we can try to work through this."

"We will see." Sheila walks away and returns to her office. She's thinking about two things: one, posing as a new employee to see who's stealing, and the other is whether she can she trust Jasmine and if it's possible, despite what's happened, for them to have some type of relationship. She's really thinking about it, and knows she cannot tell John this. In fact, she can't even understand her own feelings. She is supposed to hate this woman, for she's destroyed her life. Instead, she is finding that she has compassion for her. The only answer she has for this is God. *God must be moving in me; he is working things out despite the situation,* she thinks. *God is in complete control.* She says a quick prayer. *God, do the things that I cannot do. Speak the things that haven't been said. Repair the things that need to be mended, and restore and heal the broken heart.* Sheila's prayer is not for herself but for Jasmine.

Jasmine is feeling way too emotional and she wants to talk, so she and Jacqueline go to her mom's. They pull up and Erika opens the door to meet them. Jacqueline gets out and runs to Erika, and they hug. Jasmine also hugs her mom, and they go inside. Jacqueline goes off to play, which leaves Erika and Jasmine some time to talk. "So," Erika says, "how are things going?"

"I wish it were better. I do not want this baby to not know his father. He's a boy and there are things only a man can teach him."

"Oh Jasmine, stop it and grow up. I know you don't know a lot about your father and you may want to, and I will tell you one day but it's not today. You just need to stick to the plan. You already messed it up by getting pregnant."

"But Mom, I still don't understand what *your* plan is."

"Jasmine, you do not need to. Haven't I always come through for you?"

"Yes, Mom."

"Everything I do is for you. I know you don't

understand now but you will one day. Just trust me, Jasmine."

"Ok, Mom. I still haven't heard from John. I sent him a picture of the baby along with a 'Forget me not, Daddy' note and your letter threatening child support."

"Good. So how are things at work?"

"They're good."

"So you think Sheila got your message?"

"Yeah, I think she did. But I also think she's the reason why John hasn't contacted me."

"How do you mean?"

"I think it's his feelings for her that are in the way."

"Do you think you need to send her a message too?"

"No, not yet."

"Well, how are you so sure of that? Have you spoken with her?"

"We haven't spoken the way you may have wanted, but she is cordial and she did ask me how I was feeling the other day. But I knew she was only talking about my pregnancy. So I said a lot better, thanks for asking." Sheila stands there as if she is going to say something else, but changes her mind and walks away. Jasmine doesn't tell her mother about their last conversation because she knows she wouldn't understand.

"Oh Jasmine, that was your time to dig a jab at her."

"No, Mom, it was not."

"Jasmine, what did I tell you? You are too soft."

"Mom, I am the one who was seeing her husband. I *should* be soft. Besides, this whole thing is wrong. I do not even know why you insist that I become friends with her anyway."

"Oh, this is not about her any way, and she will see in time."

"What, this is about John?"

"You're asking too many questions."

"Mother, I'm carrying his child. I need to know."

"No, it is not about him."

"Then what is this about, Mom, and why all the secrets? I know I have not done everything you wanted me to do. Now I have fallen in love with her husband and am having his baby. I know not all this was a part of your plan and I am sorry. But Mom, I can no longer live a life following your plans. I want to change my way of living." Jasmine's tears began to fall.

"I know, but it will be all over soon. Please do not give up now, I promise you, and then you know everything. You just cannot give up now." Erika has tears in her eyes as well.

"Ok. Ok, Mom, don't cry, I won't give up. But I can't do this too much longer."

"I know, Jasmine. Thank you."

EIGHTEEN

It's the day of Bible study, and someone has pushed a large envelope under the door of Sister Rose, the pastor's secretary.

Now, Sister Rose has been a longtime, faithful member of the church. She's a little older and full of wisdom, and she's like family to many of the church members. Rose knew Pastor when he first became a minister, and when he established his own church she followed him. Rose was around when he was engaged to his wife and he cheated on her with a member of the church. Sister Rose is loyal to both Pastor and First Lady.

When Sister Rose comes in she sees the envelope, notices that it says "Confidential," and slides it under Pastor's office door. When he comes in, he sees the confidential envelope and immediately opens it. He finds another envelope and a short letter which reads: *I hope this is not what all your ministers' wives do.* After reading that, he knows that whatever's in the envelope he's not going to like. He takes a deep breath and pulls out the remaining contents from the large envelope: two pictures of Minister Carter's wife, Traci. One is of her half naked dancing on a pole, and the other is of her giving a man a lap dance.

Pastor is incredibly upset. He looks at the outer envelope for a return address but of course there is none. He goes out to Rose and asks who gave her this envelope. "No one…it was on the floor when I came in. Why, is there something wrong?"

"Well, yeah. There's no return address and the contents are disturbing."

"Oh, do you want me to find out who put it there?"

"How can you find that out?"

"We have a camera, remember. It was installed shortly after you become pastor because you were receiving anonymous mail, like this one with no return address. Just let me look for the instructions and I'll come in and help you."

"Ok, thank you."

Rose tells him the camera is set to record by motion so there's no wasted tape, and that when the tape is full it alerts her and she puts in another one. Rose helps him to get to today's date. "Ok, you can hit play now to view the tape. If you need me just call me."

Pastor hits play and sees Sister Kim Upland slide a big envelope under Rose's door and walk away. Sister Upland is one of the newer church members, one of those who like to tell everybody's business—although she's told Pastor that she only wants to keep him informed as to what's going on in the church. If this is going on, it's not good.

He calls his wife and asks her to come down early

after he explains everything. He wants to discuss how he should approach this delicate matter before he addresses it tonight.

The whole situation concerns Lady Campbell, and she prays all the way to church. When she sees her husband, she can tell he's been praying too. "This could truly damage and destroy their marriage," she says. "We have to get to the root of this. Who could be this cruel?"

Pastor says, "We need to see Sister Upland but first let's ask Rose. Ask her to come in."

Sister Rose walks in with her pen and pad in her hand. "Oh, you don't need that," Pastor says. "We just have to ask you something."

"Oh, what is it?"

"Have you heard any rumors going around?"

"Well Pastor, there's always something. Does this have to do with that envelope?"

"Yes, Rose, and it's upsetting us. Is anything going around about Traci Carter? And of course, this is confidential."

"There's talk about the fight in the parking lot, and how her husband was fighting the guy she was cheating on him with."

"Is there anything else?"

"I don't know how much this is true, but it's said that someone has pictures of her and this guy."

"Do you know who started this?"

"No."

Lady Campbell says, "Can you see if Sister Upland is here? We would like to see her."

Rose leaves and finds Sister Upland in the sanctuary. She gives her the message and she follows her to the office.

The Pastor's door is closed so she knocks. "Come in."

"Pastor you—" Sister Upland stops. "Oh hi, Lady Campbell. Y'all wanted to see me?"

"Yes, we understand that you placed this envelope under Sister Rose's door," Pastor says, holding it up. "Who gave this to you?"

"Yes I did, because you needed to know this."

"Who gave this to you?"

"The person who gave it to me is not the one who started this. And I was told to keep it under wraps."

"Can you please give us the person's name? Who started this?"

"It was Deacon Price's wife, and the talk is that Deacon used to go see Traci dance years ago and he was quite taken by her. Now that she goes to our church he is quite beside himself, and Sister Price is sick and tired of how he is acting."

"Ok, thank you. We truly appreciate all your help. You can go."

Lady Campbell says, "Wow, this has nothing to do with Traci personally. She's an unknowing victim who's being attacked because of her past by the actions of a desperate wife who's fighting to maintain her marriage."

"You sound like you know how to address this. So, after my lesson I'm going to give you the floor."

"Ok."

After Pastor's lesson on forgiveness, which was good and fitting, he turned it over to his wife. "Well, praise the Lord, saints. Pastor fed us some good meat for us to chew on. Now I'm not going to be long, but something has come to our attention that needs to be addressed and I want to say this. Whatever's being shown around, I want it to stop as well as the gossip. And let me say this. A person's past does not always represent their present or their future. That's why it's called a past, and we all have one. It represents something that once was. It's not our place to judge or condemn a person because of their past. God is the only one who can judge, and he will judge us all in the end. So saints, please be forgiving of others, because we all need forgiveness. And now, can we stand for the benediction? May the Lord watch between you and thee until we meet again. Amen."

Traci is getting Little Steven ready for church. Big Steven has already left. Sometimes he would get him ready and take him to church, but lately since he and Traci began having problems he's not helping her do anything.

When Traci gets to church, she sees that they are still doing corporate prayer. She rushes to get in on it, only to hear the tail end before everyone goes back to their seats. She takes Little Steven downstairs to children's church, and gets a little mad when she sees Sister Green in her seat. *She knows that's my seat, so why is she sitting there?* she thinks. *I know there are no assigned seats but she knows I always sit there.* So now Traci has to sit about four rows back, even though she likes to sit close to the front.

Traci is feeling good. She greets and hugs a few people around her before they do praise and worship. She hears a lot of chattering and looks around as she tries to focus on the Praise Team, and then the announcements are being read, she prepares her tithing envelope for the offering. She feels a few stares but ignores it as she walks to the table. She waves at a few friends who are sitting where she normally sits and goes back to her seat.

Just before the Pastor gives the word, the praise team sings one last song. It's one of Traci's favorites, so she immediately gets up and starts singing. She notices people are passing something around. When Sister Green turns around and looks at her, it makes her wonder if something is being passed around about her. Sister Green passes the envelope to her friend, Sister Johnson, who is sitting two rows up from Traci. Traci is breaking her neck to see what is in the envelope just as Pastor stands up before going to the podium. She's so shocked and upset when she sees a picture of herself, she doesn't realize that she's let out a loud "*No!*" Her eyes fill with blinding tears as she grabs her bag and slides out of the aisle. Her outcry gets the pastor's attention, and when he sees her leaving he rushes to the mic and calls her name. Traci stops for a second but is so embarrassed she continues on.

At that point Steven gets up, wondering what's going on. He tries to make his way to Traci, and so does Lady Campbell. Traci is walking towards the door, planning to get Little Steven and leave. As she reaches the vestibule, Big Steven calls out to her and she stops. "What's wrong?" he says as he walks towards her.

"They're passing around pictures of me," Traci says, crying.

Now Steven is alarmed. "What pictures?"

"One of me dancing at the adult club. Someone's found out what I used to do."

Lady Campbell also comes out. "Are you ok?"

"No. Someone has passed around a picture of me

dancing at the adult club—someone knows about my past."

Lady Campbell says, "Traci do not let them win. That was your past, that is not who you are now. Stay so we—I mean, Pastor and I—can address this." Steven is so livid he's pacing the floor. This has always been one of his fears, and he doesn't know how to react.

Inside the sanctuary, Pastor thanks the praise team and says, "I'm calling a mandatory meeting for members only immediately after service." Of course, that starts a little chatter and then he begins to sing "Yess—Lord.   Yess—Lord—yess—Lord—yess—Lord." He sings this for about 10 minutes until he feels the presence of the Lord.

Out in the vestibule, Lady Campbell also feels God's presence. "God is here; let's go back inside." She grabs Traci's hand. They all walk back in. Pastor sees them and, feeling moved by the Spirit, tells the church to quickly come to the altar. He continues to sing.

As the people cry out to God at the altar, Traci and Steven go up. Pastor prays and then he comes down. As the Lord leads him, he lays hands on some as he walks through the people, and the Spirit heightens. He lays hands on Traci and Steven, then he returns to the podium and watches his flock. When he feels the Spirit lifting, he tells them to return to their seats. As they go back he says, "It looks like God has changed the order of the service, so I'll save my sermon for next week. I'm gonna give the benediction and let y'all go to the restroom. It's now 12:15, so I expect everyone back by 12:30. Adult members only, everyone else can wait in the lounge."

Once everyone is back, Lady Campbell starts off with prayer. Traci and Steven are there, as well. After prayer, Pastor steps up to the podium. "On Wednesday, Lady Campbell addressed an issue and I thought it was over. But someone is being vicious and has passed around something that is very hurtful and damaging about another member's past. I want it to stop now. Again, a person's past does not always represent who they are now. We are too quick to pass our little judgments on someone without having all the facts. You are slandering someone's reputation, and truthfully, you could be sued for defamation of character. I would advise you to deal with your own issues, and if you need help come to my wife and me. And stop meddling in other people's business. I should make you stand up and apologize to the person you're victimizing, but if I hear anything about this again I *will* call you out. We are supposed to be a family unit, and we're acting like we're not hurting our sister. So, fix it before God fixes you." Pastor prays and says, "You are dismissed."

There is quiet chatter, with some asking, "What's going on?" Others are saying, "*Wow,* Pastor was mad!" Those that knew what he was talking about and were alarmed at his sternness asked, "How did it get to him?"

Traci gets up, immediately goes to get Little Steven, and leaves.

NINETEEN

When church lets out, Steven doesn't go looking for Traci. Instead, he speaks briefly to one of the ministers and then leaves, but he doesn't go home. His biggest fear has just happened: the church knows about his wife's past and he's embarrassed. He doesn't know how to deal with his feelings of anger, and he's not sure what he's going to do. All he knows is that he can't go home, so he drives aimlessly around until he finds himself in front of the Marriott Hotel. He checks in, telling himself he just needs some time away to clear his head. He also needs to know what the private investigator has found. *Traci said she would not see him again, but the private investigator will tell me the truth,* he thinks.

In his 25th-floor hotel room, Steven tries to look out at the view but he can't because he keeps seeing images of Traci with this guy—the guy that the old Steven wants to kill, because he's the reason that he's in this situation. He kneels down beside the bed to pray, but he can't find any words except, *Oh God, please help me.* He stays there for about 15 minutes until, feeling defeated, he gets up. Pastor comes to his mind, so he calls him.

"Hello?"

"Hi Pastor, it's Steven Carter."

"Yes Steven, I know your voice."

"Oh. I'm sorry to bother you, but what happened today has really gotten to me more than I thought it would. And I can't go home, so I got a room at the Marriott Hotel."

"Does Traci know where you're at?"

"No, I still don't have anything to say to her. And I'm just waiting to hear from the private investigator I hired."

"Wait a minute. You hired a private investigator on Traci?"

"Yeah, it was right after I caught her and I told her not to see him again. She said she wouldn't, but I don't trust her...that's why I hired a private investigator."

"Now Steven, I agree that this is quite a blow and it may be hard to shake it off. But man, you can't tell me you don't love Traci. And I know you're struggling, but if you were done with her you would have been gone. I don't care what this investigator finds, it won't change the fact that you still love your wife. And let me tell you this: Jesus endured our burdens as he bore the cross, so we also have a cross to bear. Maybe this is part of your cross that you have to bear. And believe me, you're not alone. Now I can't tell you what to do, but I suggest you don't make any hasty decisions before praying about it."

"I did try before I called you, but I couldn't."

"That's because you're not giving it to him. Steven, you know what to do—get out of yourself, open your heart to God, and give him your pain. Then your words will come. You can't hold this, because it will destroy you."

"I know you're right, Pastor, but I can't guarantee my reaction if she sees him again. I'm trying to maintain my Christian walk, Pastor, but the old me is trying to come out."

"Well, I'm praying that God sustains you and you seek his guidance. And remember, Steven, God can do anything. He'll see you through this, just let him have his way."

"Yes Pastor, I will. And thank you for your help and advice. Have a good evening." After hanging up, Steven is able to pray. But his phone keeps ringing, and after looking several times and seeing that it's Traci he ignores it.

Steven, not intending to go home, enjoys his alone time at the hotel. He watches TV, and when he starts getting hungry he orders room service. He spends the night and then gets up early in the morning, takes a shower, and heads home to change his clothes and go to work.

When he arrives home, Traci is up but Little Steven is still asleep. He peeks in on him and then goes into the bedroom he used to share with Traci to get something to put on for work.

Traci had been calling him almost all night. She was afraid that he'd left her but now that he's home she's still afraid. At first, she watches him as he moves around the room, waiting to see if he's going to say anything. Of course he doesn't, so she says, "Steven, where were you last night? Why were you ignoring my calls? Baby, please stop this and talk to me." She goes over to him and stands directly in his face. He tries to move around her but she won't let him.

"Move, Traci. I'm not playing with you."

"No, we need to talk. I'm not moving."

He tries to get around her again but she still blocks him, so he pushes her but still can't get by her. Angry now, Steven pushes her harder than he intends. Traci falls backward, stumbles over a nearby closet foot stool, and lands hard on her side. She had put her hand out to stop her fall and now she's badly hurt her wrist.

Steven sees her fall and tries to catch her, but after she fell he thinks she's all right and he continues getting ready for work, and leaves.

TWENTY

Paul is missing Traci badly, and he wants to see her. But first, he has to call Jasmine so he can see his daughter Jacqueline, whom he hasn't seen lately because he's been so caught up in Traci.

He calls Jasmine and she answers on the first ring. "Hello?"

"Hey Jazz, you answered the phone quickly. Are you ok?"

"Yeah, I thought you were John."

"Who?"

"You know, the father of the child I am carrying."

"Oh, that's right, I forgot you're pregnant. So, how's everything?"

"To tell you the truth, Paul, things are not as I expected them to be. John isn't coming around and I haven't talked to him. I saw him once when he went to my doctor's appointment, and that was only because he didn't believe that I was pregnant. That was last month."

"He sees that you're pregnant and he's still not coming around? What is wrong with him?"

"Well, he told me he never wanted kids and I guess he is proving it. The thing I don't understand is that I could tell he was excited. But I think his feelings for her are in the way, and it's stopping him from everything. It hurts to know that he's going to miss experiencing this with me."

"Yeah well, I was there with you with Jacqueline and we had our moments. Nevertheless, to have Jacqueline now it was worth it all—and that's mainly why I was calling. I want to see her this Saturday."

"Sure, what time should I have her ready?"

"I'll get her at 11:00 and bring her back around two or three o'clock. Is that ok?"

"Yeah, that's fine."

"Ok. So what do I say to Jacqueline if she starts asking me questions about you? What did you tell her?"

"I told her that I'm going to have a baby and that she is going to be a big sister. She seemed to be excited. She asked me if the baby got in my stomach the way you and I made her. I said yes, but that Mr. John and I made this baby. I know she doesn't understand it, but that's what I told her."

"Ok, I just wanted to know what to say if she asks me anything. All right, then I will see you on Saturday."

After hanging up with Jasmine, Paul decides to call Traci to see if he can see her, but her phone just rings and she doesn't answer. *I'll try again a little later,* he thinks, figuring that perhaps she is on her work break. He's been trying to give Traci some time to work on things with her husband, but he can't deny his feelings for her any longer. When he tries to call her again, she still doesn't answer so he calls her job and is told that she's out for three weeks. Paul thinks either she took off to spend time with her husband or that something is wrong.

Now his adrenaline is running, and he paces the floor trying to figure out what to do. He decides to drive over to her house to see if her car is there. It's there but her husband's is not, and he wonders if they went away in his car.

Paul sits there in his car for a half an hour, thinking that she could be in there. Her husband could have gone away or maybe is at work. All these thoughts are driving him crazy, until he says, "Forget it, I'm knocking on her door—I don't care. I just need to see her."

He gets out of the car, which is parked across the street near the corner, and he walks to her house. He rings the doorbell, ready for whoever opens the door but wishing it would be Traci. He waits a few minutes, rings it again, then waits and tries one more time before the door opens and Traci appears with her arm in a sling. "Oh, Traci! Baby, what happened? I was so worried about you; that's why I came over. Did he do this to you?"

"Uh, yes and no."

"What do you mean 'yes and no'? Baby, what happened?"

"I was blocking his way trying to get him to talk to me after he stayed out all night on Sunday. He pushed me, I stumbled over something, and in trying to brace myself from the fall, I sprained my wrist."

"Where is he?"

"He's at work."

"Let me in, Traci."

"Paul, you can't."

"Traci, you and I both know he's not coming home soon. I'm coming in." She steps aside and closes the door.

"Paul, these past few weeks have been hard."

"What did he do besides push you?"

"No, it wasn't him. I went to church two weeks ago and someone was passing around pictures of me. I only saw one, a picture of me dancing on the pole. I hollered out 'No!' but I did not mean to and I left. Because of that, Steven stayed out all night. So you see, I was confronting him as to his whereabouts. He's still not talking to me."

"Traci, how much more are you going to take from him?"

"Paul don't do this. I can't leave."

"What, you want him to hurt you again?"

"No."

"He's already hurting you mentally by ignoring you and now physically. Look Traci, this man doesn't want you. But I want you, and I can no longer stand on the sidelines and watch him make a fool out of you. You deserve better—you deserve *me*." He gently grabs her by her shoulders and kisses her. Releasing her, he says, "You don't get it, you just don't know what you've done to me. I started falling for you back then and that's why I was coming to the club every day requesting you to dance for me. It wasn't about your dancing—well, at first it was, but then we had some stimulating conversations. I like how you think, and plus I knew you were different from those other girls. Traci, I'm not saying I'm better than your husband, but from all the conversations we had I connected with you, and not every man can connect with a woman on an intellectual level like I've connected with you. The only regret I have is that you're married and you're not happy. I don't want him to hurt you again. Just come with me now, Traci."

"Paul you know I can't leave and especially without my child. You'd better leave before he comes home."

"I don't care if he comes home. I *want* him to come home. I keep on telling you, I'm not playing here. I want you for myself. Oh baby, I don't mean to scare you but I want you to know how serious I am. You're his for now but you *will* be mine." Traci starts to walk towards the door, hoping he'll follow her. He does, just as the door opens and in walks Steven.

Steven's solemn look turns to anger. "You brought him into our house?"

"Steven, no. The doorbell rang and when I opened it he was there."

"And so you just let him in?"

"He just—"

Cutting her off, he says, "I don't want to hear it, Traci." Looking at Paul, he says, "You don't give up, do you?" What, you're ready for some more?"

Paul says, "You're not going to talk to her like that in front of me."

"This is my wife and I talk to her any way I please."

"Yeah well, not for long if I can help it." Steven just steps up and punches him in the face. But Paul is ready and as he sees him coming closer, he swings and hits him as well, and they start fighting in the entryway.

Traci is afraid that someone is going to get seriously hurt, so she runs to get the phone and calls the police. In a panicked voice, she says, "Help! They're fighting in my house!"

"Who's fighting, ma'am?"

"My husband is fighting the man I was seeing!"

"And he's in your house?"

"Yes! Please hurry, come quickly."

"Ok ma'am, what is your address?"

She gives it and then hangs up, hollering, "Stop it! I've called the police. Please, stop!" Paul is about to take another swing but when he hears her, he stops and heads for the door. He doesn't want to be arrested again. "This isn't over." He looks at Traci and adds, "I'm fighting for you."

Steven, bruised a little, says, "What does that mean?" He looks at Traci.

"Steven, I really don't know. I was lying in bed, the doorbell kept on ringing, and when I opened the door he was standing there. And when he saw my arm in the sling he asked what happened. He kind of walked in and I was trying to get him to leave when you walked in."

"Did you give him our address?"

"No! I would never do that."

"So how does he know where we live?"

"I don't know…maybe he followed us home the day you saw us together. You must believe I would never tell him where we live."

"I thought I saw him follow you the other week when you went to the store."

"What? Well, why didn't you tell me?" *Traci is too afraid to tell him the truth, that he called her saying that he was outside that he followed them the day he caught them.*

"Because I wasn't sure if you planned to have him meet you here, and I had you investigated. I called someone right after I caught you with him. I just couldn't trust you."

"You had me followed?"

"Yeah, I did."

"So, what did you find?"

"Well, ah, nothing. Look, this whole thing is hard to deal with as it is, and now the church knows and there are pictures."

"This isn't easy for me either, Steven. I know I've made a big mistake and I should have talked to you about my feelings before I got involved with this guy. But when you found out you made it more difficult, almost unmanageable. You shut down on me and stopped speaking to me altogether."

"I know, but now you know what I was going through. It's still hard and it's going to take time for me to be able to trust you again."

"Can we please try to work on everything, including you balancing your time?"

"I'll try, but you have to tell me if he contacts you or if you see him. Ok, I will I promise."

TWENTY-ONE

When Paul gets home, he nurses his wounds as well as his ego. He's angry because he came home without Traci, and seeing her like that has made him more determined to have her. He thinks about her all the time, wondering what she's doing and hoping she's ok. He rides by her house at different times of the day and night trying to see her, and a few times he did she was with her son. But that's no longer enough for him. He needs more; he needs *her*. He doesn't want her child, only her, but if that what it takes to get her then so be it.

When Paul gets up the next day, the first thing he does is call Traci but there's no answer. He gets a shower, gets dressed, and drives by her house, still calling all the way there. He gets to her block and slowly rides by the house. When he sees both cars there, his mind begins racing. Did Steven hurt her again, or did they make up and she's lying right now in his arms? All the wondering is driving him crazy, and he has to see if he can see her. He parks around the corner at the back of the houses. He slowly walks to the back of her house and peeks into her window, trying to get a glimpse of her without being seen. It's hard to see because of the sunlight, so he decides to leave and come back when it is dark.

He's been trying to reach Traci all day, and she's still not answering his calls. Now he's on his way to find out why. He pulls up to the back of her house, walks over to her house from the side street, and peeks in her window. He gets excited when he sees her in the kitchen looking in the refrigerator—until Steven walks into the kitchen and he sees the way she looks at him. As Paul looks on with rage, he draws a fist and punches the window, causing it to crack. The noise gets their attention. With his fist bleeding, Paul ducks along the side of the house.

When Steven comes out to check, he sees blood on the window. He tells Traci, "Something must have flown into the window and it's bleeding, but it didn't die."

Paul goes back to the window, and once again sees Steven and Traci together. This time he picks up a potted plant, throws it at the window, and then runs to his car. The crashing sound scares Traci and she hollers out. Steven rushes to open the door, walks outside, and sees the shattered window. He looks around and sees a car starting to pulling off from the side street. Paul gets into his car, and as he starts to pull off he looks and sees Steven. He pauses, and then pulls off.

Steven goes in the house. "Traci!"

She comes into the room. "What's wrong? What did that?"

"That was *him*, he did that. I'm telling you now you'd better not see him again. And if I catch him he's a dead man. Now he's done crossed the line when he comes to my house. I'm not playing with him or you."

"Steven I'm scared. He won't stop…it's like he's obsessed."

"Traci, this is serious. Now tell me everything you know about him."

"Truthfully, it's not much. His name is Paul Turner, and he is an investment advisor. I forget which bank but he works for one of the largest firms. He has a five-year-old daughter. He was having some problems with his baby's mother about her boyfriend being around his daughter. Oh, and he did say when he first moved away from them that he would always drive by the house, but he said it was because he still wanted to protect them. Now I see that he's possessive and obsessive."

Paul arrives home, feeling that should hurt Steven in the pocket some. *Traci should already know that I'm not playing,* he thinks. *I told her that I love her and she said she loved me too. So what more do I have to do for her to believe me? She's mine and I will have her real soon.*

He goes into the kitchen, gets a baggie, puts some ice cubes in it and holds it to his knuckles to stop the swelling. Then he gets a bottle of water and takes it upstairs. He goes into the medicine cabinet, takes two Aleve, and goes to bed.

TWENTY-TWO

"Hello?"

"Hey Sheila, it's Traci. Girl, we need to talk."

"I know. Do you want to come over? We can order something to eat."

"Ok, I'm on my way."

When Traci gets to Sheila's house, they sit in the living room. Traci begins telling Sheila what's gotten her so upset. "I went to church on Sunday, and you know how I like sitting up front. Well, Sister Green was sitting in my seat so I had to sit about four rows back. And during service I noticed a few stares but I ignored them, until I noticed something was being passed around. When Sister Green saw what it was she turned to look at me. I had been standing up because the praise team was singing one of my favorite songs. Sister Green had passed this envelope to Sister Johnson, who was sitting two rows in front of me. Now I was breaking my neck to see what was being passed around. To my shock it was pictures of me dancing on the pole. I cried out a loud '*No*,' not realizing that I did. I grabbed my purse and was leaving the pew with eyes full of tears. Pastor called out to me, and I stopped for a moment, looked his way, and then continued. Girl, I was so hurt and embarrassed. First the fight in the parking lot and now someone is trying to publicly expose my past. And of course, this is not going to help my marriage. Then Pastor called a mandatory meeting after church to discuss this. Apparently he mentioned this in Bible study on Wednesday, but someone was determined to make my past known."

"Oh girl, I'm sorry. Did you go to the meeting?"

"I had to. It was hard, but I sat in the back. When it was over I got Little Steven and left."

"Do you have any idea who's doing this?"

"None at all. I think someone saw the fight and recognized the other man, then made the connection to me because they had pictures of me and him. I don't know."

"Does Steven know?"

"Yeah, because I drew attention to myself and Pastor called me out. Then Steven got up and met me in the vestibule and I told him what happened. He was livid because he feared this would happen. Then Lady Campbell came out. So that's why I needed to talk. I'm embarrassed and stressed because Steven didn't come home that night. I was so scared, I kept on calling him but he wouldn't answer. I didn't know what to think. I thought he left me. But when he did come home, he still wasn't talking to me. And now I've been tiptoeing around him."

"What, is it any better now?"

"No, he's still not talking to me."

"And what's this, you saw Paul again?"

"Yeah only once...I met him at the park. He said he still loves me and wants me."

"And what do *you* want?"

"Honestly, I'm torn. I want my family but I'm not sure Steven will ever forgive me. But I also want Paul…he always stimulated my mind."

"So what are you saying, Traci?"

"Well, I told Paul I need to try to make my marriage work. He asked how long. I said at least a few months, but I don't know. I told him that if I do move in with him I don't want to lose my child. He said we'll think of something."

"Oh, wow. Y'all are doing some serious talking."

"Yes, we are. I have some deep feelings for him. And Steven is drifting away from me. It's been two months and he's still not speaking to me. He acts as if I'm not there. So what if I'm not really there?"

"Oh girl, you know he's just hurt."

"Yeah, but Sheila, this is different. He never acted like this before. I really hurt him this time and I feel that I might have lost him. He stays in the basement isolated from us. In our counseling session, he told them he has nothing to say to me and that he does love me but he doesn't know what he wants. And do you know Little Steven asked me why Daddy stays in the basement?"

"No, girl, what did you tell him?"

"I didn't know what to say, girl, so I told him to ask his father. He caught me off guard. And Paul told me that my son knows something's going on because kids feel our emotions. And seriously I don't know if I can go back to church."

"Now you know Pastor and Lady Campbell are not going to allow you to leave."

"I know, but I'm embarrassed. Maybe I'll wait until things die down and then come back. I don't need this added pressure. But enough about me. What's going on with you?"

Sheila says, "Well, my life is a soap opera. The woman John was seeing just happens to be my receptionist."

"What! No, wait—tell me you didn't investigate him?"

"No, but my receptionist Jasmine, who used to be my dentist's receptionist, told me she was looking for a new job and I helped her to get this job. We were starting to become close. She told me about her boyfriend and how he's a keeper, and then one day I asked her how was she feeling because she had been out for a few days. I also asked about her friend, and she started crying saying that she hadn't heard from him in weeks and she thinks she might have caught the stomach virus. I asked her if she was pregnant, and long story short, she *is* pregnant and she still hasn't heard from him. So I told her I'd help her do a stakeout so she can confront him.

"While waiting at his apartment complex, I thought to myself how John lives there and I wondered if I would see him. A few minutes later a truck pulls up and we both speak at the same time. I was saying, 'John,' and she said, "That's him,' and we both looked at each other. I hopped out of her car and a few minutes later she did too. John had just gotten out of his truck and started walking as I was coming toward him. When he saw me he was shocked to see me. And then Jasmine walks up and stands there crying. And John said, 'What's this, y'all setting me up?' And in the end Jasmine tells him she's pregnant. And he walks back to his truck and I followed him and we left her standing there alone.

"Now I have to work with her and watch her carry his child, and I wish it was me. Now, all that happened on Friday. Now when I go back to work I get there early to avoid her because I haven't taken my position in all of this yet. I get off the elevator and she's there. Of course, I'm shocked. I couldn't say a word so I hurried to my office and wondered to myself why she was there so early. She wasn't doing overtime or making up any time. So, I swear she's trying to send me a message."

"A message like what?"

"It's like I told John, she knows I'm hurt and mad at him and that eventually I'll take my position and end up viewing her as the other woman, the one who caused my pain and the one I'll have to face every day. So, I think she's taking her position and telling me, 'I'm here and I'm not going nowhere.' And the crazy thing is, during our talks I told her things about my marriage and she told me about her relationships with men and what she wants. I even told her she should talk to Pastor and Lady Campbell about her current situation. I gave her the church number." Just then the doorbell rings. "Our foods here," Sheila says.

While eating in the kitchen Traci says, "Boy, I never would have seen myself in this situation."

Sheila says, "Yeah, me either. But we're in it and it's going to take God to get us through it."

TWENTY-THREE

Paul hasn't heard from Traci in a week and he knows it's because of her husband. *He's keeping her from calling me,* he thinks. *He probably threatens her with taking their son if she contacts me. I've got to think of something; she needs me.*

He calls her cell phone over and over again. First, he says, "Hi Traci, it's me…give me a call." Then, "Call me, it's Paul," and then, "Just call me back, Traci. I want to know if you're ok." And then, "Traci, stop annoying me. Pick up the phone now." Then the last call is, "Traci, baby, I'm sorry. I'm just worried about you. Please just pick up. You better not let him have you, you're mine. Traci, I love you." He doesn't stop calling, and he doesn't care what time of day or night it is. He needs to hear from her, needs her attention. But she isn't giving it, and that drives him crazy. Finally, he drives to her house. *I'm so close to my dream becoming a reality,* he thinks, *and he's not going to mess this up. I had better not see him near her or I will do more than bust out the window.*

He drives down the side street, parks, casually gets out and walks along the back of the houses until he gets to hers. He looks in the window. He thinks he just saw her but he doesn't have a good view, so he moves a little further over and stands on a large flower pot underneath the kitchen window. Boldly, he looks in. He isn't thinking about being seen, he's only focused on seeing her.

Then she comes into view, and he watches her every move. *She's so beautiful,* he thinks. Suddenly she turns and faces his direction, as if she knows he's there. He locks in on her beauty—her hair, her face, and the lips he longs to kiss. Then she turns and walks away.

As Paul moves to keep her in view, his foot slips. He falls onto the glass patio table, breaking it. He gets up and starts to run, but he stops and slowly walks away, not wanting to be seen.

This time, it's Traci who comes out. It takes him by surprise as he stops in his tracks. "Oh, baby, it's you. I just wanted to see you. I miss you."

"Paul, you have to stop this. You have to go now…he's going to call the cops on you."

"I don't care, Traci. Come with me now. I need you; I know he is keeping you from calling me."

"What are you talking about?"

"I know he probably threatened you and that's why I haven't heard from you."

"No, Paul, he has not. I've told you I'm working on my marriage."

"So he hasn't threatened you?"

"No, we're working it out."

"So you no longer want to be with me, is that what you are saying?"

"Yes."

Paul walks closer to her in disbelief. "He's gotten

to you."

"Paul, he is my husband. I'm sorry about us. It shouldn't have happened."

Paul shakes his head. "Don't say that." He grabs her.

"Let me go, Paul!" As he tightens his grip on her, she begins to holler for Steven.

Steven, unaware of what's going on, is coming up the basement stairs when he hears Traci calling him from the patio. He goes outside and is surprised to find that guy with his arm around his wife, and it causes Steven to snap. He's tired of this guy invading their privacy, and it is time for him to take matters into his own hands and protect his family.

Steven steps up to Paul. "Let her go!"

"No! She's mine and I'm not leaving without her."

Traci's eyes grow big with fear. Steven sees it and knows he needs to act now, because there's no way he is letting him leave with his wife. Acting fast and running on adrenaline, Steven knows he has to run the risk of hitting Traci as he quickly punches Paul in the head, hoping that the blow will make him let her go in order to protect himself. But Paul doesn't let her go at first, so Steven punches him a few more times until he finally releases her and they begin to fight.

Traci runs into the house, quickly calls the police, and then comes back outside. "The cops are on their way!" She hopes Paul will just leave, but they continue to fight. They're both bleeding badly, and Traci pleads for them to stop. The patio furniture doesn't stop them from fighting; they just fall onto it. Traci's hollering and sounds of the patio furniture crashing finally cause the neighbors to come out. They try to break them up, but no avail. The more Steven says, "Leave my wife alone!" the angrier they both become.

Somehow, Paul gets Steven down on the ground and begins stomping on him, and their fight turns into a street brawl. Steven manages to grab his leg and yanks it, causing Paul to fall hard and hit his head. Suddenly, police sirens could be heard in the distance.

When the cops arrive, Traci explains everything because both men are too hurt to give a full statement. An ambulance also arrives but has to call for another one, as both Steven and Paul are bad off. A paramedic examines Steven." "He seems to have broken ribs, a broken nose and both of his eyes are swollen shut. Paul may have a concussion from the fall and the punches to his head. His eyes are also swollen shut, and he has a broken nose as well." The ambulances take them both to the same hospital. Traci tells the drivers she'll meet them there, then goes into the house and grabs her cell phone, charger and bag. She sets the alarm on in the house and drives to the hospital. The police are at the hospital as well, and Traci is asked if she wants to press charges. She's reluctant to answer, so she asks if she can deal with this later. They give her a copy of the police report.

The doctors work on Steven while Traci is at the admissions desk filling out paperwork. She's just finished Steven's when she hears a nurse call out, "Who is here with Paul Turner?"

"I guess I am for now," Traci answers, and the nurse asks her to fill out his paperwork. "Oh, I know him but I don't know his information."

"That's ok, we copied his insurance card from his wallet. All we need is your signature of authorization to treat his injuries."

"What are they?"

"It looks like he has a concussion and a broken nose. His eyes are swollen shut so we can't tell if there are broken vessels or damage to the eyes itself."

"Oh, I guess I can do that."

"Are you his girlfriend?"

"No, I'm an acquaintance."

"Ok, well we'll can do what we can for him but can you notify someone that he's here so we can get proper authorization? And here are his belongings." Traci is given Steven's things and now she has Paul's too.

In the waiting room, a doctor comes to her and explains what's going on with Steven. "During their examination, his stomach seems to be swollen so we're going to take an x-ray to see if he has internal bleeding. If so, we would have to go inside to find what's bleeding and repair it. When I'm done, I'll come back here and let you know how he's doing."

"Ok. Thank you, Doctor."

"You're welcome."

Traci takes out Paul's wallet, looking for anything that will help her figure out who to call. She finds that he has $2000 in the billfold and wonders if he always carries that much money on him. Behind his license, she finds a picture of a woman and a little girl. Turning it over, she sees that it reads, "Jasmine and Jacqueline, 5 years old." *Oh, this must be his daughter and her mother,* she thinks. *This is the one he was talking about.* Staring at her picture, Traci thinks that Jasmine isn't bad looking. She starts to grab his phone to find her number when another doctor comes in. "Who is here with Paul Turner?"

"I am," Traci says.

The doctor sits down next to her. "Did Mr. Turner pass out when he fell?"

"He might have. I remember him trying to get up, but then he laid back down and he didn't get back up. I was busy attending to my husband."

"Oh. Well, who are you to Mr. Turner, then?"

"I'm an acquaintance. I was just trying to find someone to call and tell them he's here."

"But I can come to you until someone else comes?"

"Yes."

"You stated that Mr. Turner was in a fight with your husband, Mr. Carter. Did I hear that right?"

"Yes."

"He's been unconscious since he came in, and we're waiting for him to wake up. He has a broken nose, which we are going to fix. His eyes look bad but we can't tell how badly until he wakes up. That's it for now. I'll come back with any changes."

"Ok. Thank you, Doctor." Traci goes back to Paul's phone, hoping it doesn't have a password. It doesn't, so she goes to the J's in his contacts until she finds a Jasmine. Before calling, she tries to think of what she going to say.

"Hello?"

"Hello, is this Jasmine?"

"Yes, who is this?"

"My name is Traci, and I'm an acquaintance of Paul. I'm calling you from his phone because he has been hurt and he is in the hospital, Lincoln Hospital. Can you come down?"

"Yes, I'll be there. Is he ok?"

"I believe so, but I'll explain everything to you when you get here."

TWENTY-FOUR

John is home relaxing when he pulls out the picture of Jasmine's ultrasound. Each time he looks at it, he remembers the sound of the baby's heartbeat and he cannot help but think, *Wow, this is my baby.* As he stares at it he begins to think, *I don't want him to be like me and not know his father.* He shakes his head. *Yeah, I want to be in his life.* He grabs his phone and calls Jasmine.

Jasmine's phone suddenly rings and she slightly jumps. She answers it, thinking it is her mom. "Mom, I'll call you back."

"Jasmine, it's John."

Jasmine's heart leaps. "John, I'm sorry. Hi."

"Hey, do you need to call me back?"

"No, its fine. I can talk for a few minutes."

"Are you ok? What is that noise?"

"I am at the hospital."

"What? Is the baby ok? Are you ok? Should I come down?"

"What? Oh no, I'm fine, John. My daughter's father was in a fight and he has a concussion and other things but he is stable."

"That's good. So, I was calling you to see if we can talk in person."

"When and where?"

"Is tomorrow too soon? At your place?"

"That's fine. I'll see you tomorrow."

"Ok. I hope your daughter's father will be ok."

"Thanks, John. See you." John hangs up feeling hopeful. Now he has to get his words together so he can explain his actions to her and how this baby is making him feel. He's also thinking about Sheila, so he calls her.

"Hello?"

"Hi Sheila, how are you doing?"

"Oh hi, John. I am doing."

"What does that mean?"

"John, I'll be ok. I'm just hurt. My love for you is still strong but I just need more time to heal and then I can move on. But right now, it is just hard now that I know it's really over for us. I guess this baby has really changed you."

"Yeah, I guess so. I didn't know that would be possible, you know, with my issues of not having a father. To me it's a lot of responsibility, but I can't allow my child to go without a father. I'm still not sure how things will work out but I am going to take it slow. It is not as if I am moving in with her. I am just going to attempt to resume a relationship with her. I really don't know what else to say that will make you feel any better. But you must know that I will be here for you no matter what."

"The other night didn't mean anything to you?"

"Yes it did, Sheila, but I can't have a child in this world without me being there."

"You can be there for your child without being

with her—unless there's something else you are not telling me. John, a child doesn't make a relationship work. And you know I still love you."

"Well Sheila, I have to go. I love you too and I'll be calling you, and you call me if you need anything."

"Ok John. I'll talk to you later."

Feeling awful, John hangs up. But he knows he has to follow his heart…or at least try.

THE END

COMING SOON!

COMING OUT OF HIS SHADOW: PART II

ONE

While sitting in the waiting room, Traci starts to takes her phone out to call Sheila, but when the doctor comes in she puts her phone back in her bag. "Mrs. Carter?"

"Yes."

"Mr. Carter is back in his room. We gave him a chest x-ray and an MRI. They both show that he has broken ribs on his left side, which will heal on its own within eight weeks, and that he also has badly bruised his spleen."

"Spleen!"

"Yes, it's under the rib cage. And as you know, he has a broken nose and his eyes are swollen. We fixed his nose and started putting ice on his eyes. He will be admitted to the hospital and when there's a bed available he will be taken to his room. He'll look bad to you; he's bruised, swollen and in pain but in time he'll heal. Do you have any questions?"

"How long will he stay in the hospital?"

"It could be three to six weeks so we can monitor his condition because of his spleen, and so he can receive fluids and pain medication. Anything else?"

"No."

"Then you can go see him now. But I must tell you he is pretty swollen, and he's also hooked up to the machine. He may not wake up for another 20 minutes or so."

"Ok. Thank you so much, Doctor." She lets out a big sigh of relief.

Jasmine says, "I wish Paul's doctor would hurry up and tell me something."

Just then the door opens and someone says, "Is there a Ms. Carter here?"

Traci says yes, but then she says, "But this is Jasmine, Paul Turner's…" She turns to Jasmine.

"Hi, I'm Jasmine Anderson, Mr. Turner's ex and his daughter's mother. I guess I'm next of kin."

"Ok. Ms. Anderson, Mr. Turner came in here unconscious, but he's awake now and a little groggy. We fixed his nose and put ice packs on his eyes for the swelling. He doesn't know what happened and why he's here. He knows his name but he has some memory loss. To determine the extent of his memory loss we need to keep him here for observation because of his concussion."

"For how long?"

"Well, that depends on what he remembers. I want you to both come and see him now."

Jasmine says, "Together?"

"No, one at a time."

Jasmine says, "I'll go first." She gets up.

The doctor tells Traci to come too but to just wait in the hallway. "I want to see who he recognizes and what he says."

Jasmine slowly walks into Paul's room. "Oh Paul, how do you feel?"

He looks at her. "Do I know you?"

Jasmine is hurt that he doesn't recognize her but tries not to show it. "Paul, it is me, Jasmine. We have a five-year-old together. Do you remember your daughter Jacqueline?"

"No, I don't. Is this some kind of joke? Where is my wife, Traci? I want to see Traci."

Jasmine can't help but cry. She turns and walks towards the doctor who's at the door and says, "I don't understand this. He's not married. She's married to another guy and they were having an affair."

"So, with that it seems he may have lost his long-term memory for the moment and remembers only what he believed was true. It depends on his state of mind. Let's bring Traci in and see how he responds to her."

Traci walks in and see's Jasmine crying. She looks at Paul with his nose bandaged and his eyes barely opened. "How is he?"

Paul says, "Happy to see you, Baby. Baby, tell me what happened. Why am I here?"

Confused, Traci looks away from Paul to the doctor. He nods his head. "Paul you were in a fight and you hit your head," she says.

"Oh, well that explains my headache. Who and why was I fighting?"

The doctor says, "Do you remember anything?"

"No."

"Ok, well we don't want to overwhelm you with things. But it looks like you have a concussion of some sort and you're a little mixed up right now. So, let's just give it a few days and see if things come back to you."

"Ok but can I just talk to my wife for a few minutes?"

"Not right now, you need to rest." The doctor gestures for Jasmine and Traci to leave the room, but Paul says, "Traci, wait! Don't leave yet."

"It's ok, Paul. I'll be here." Traci leaves the room, very concerned.

When they are away from Paul's room Traci says to the doctor, "I thought when you have a concussion you just lose your memory. Why does he think I am his wife?"

"There have only been a few cases like this and it's based on the person's state of mind when the injury occurred. So, this is important: do either one of you know what state of mind Mr. Turner has been in these few months?" Once again, Traci explains everything to the doctor.

The doctor says, "He's exhibiting the exact type of behavior I mentioned. His mind strongly believes that you are his wife. All we can do now is wait to see when it returns."

Traci and Jasmine both thank the doctor and he walks away. Traci says, "Wow…when it rains it pours."

"Yeah, tell me about it."

Traci says, "I'm going to check on my husband for a little bit. Are you still going to be here?"

"Yeah, I'm going to the waiting room and call my mom."

"I'll see you in there." Traci goes to the nurses' station and asks to see her husband in recovery.

"What's his name?" the nurse asks.

"Steven Carter."

"He's in Room 426."

"Thank you," Traci says, and goes to his room. He looks worse than Paul, but she thanks God that he's still alive as tears fill her eyes.

Steven hears her. He opens his eyes and tries to speak. "Don't talk," Traci says. "Save your strength."

He says in a low voice, "I'm sorry. I love you." He wrenches in pain.

With tears in her eyes, Traci bends over to kiss him. "I love you too. Now get some rest. You've been through a lot. I'll be back tomorrow." She walks into the waiting room and sees Jasmine on the phone. Jasmine signals for her to sit next to her. Traci hears her say, "Thanks, Mom. I'll see you sometime tomorrow," before she hangs up.

Jasmine turns to Traci. "How is your husband?"

"He's awake and in a lot of pain. He looks bad with those things hooked up to the machine. But I thank God he's alive."

"Well, I say amen to that."

"I hope Paul's memory comes back soon."

"I do too, because I don't know how to explain this to our daughter."

Traci says, "I know, I have to tell my son. Well, I'm going home and try to get some rest. I have to call my mother-in-law."

"Ok, I'll see you tomorrow."

When Traci gets home from the hospital, the first thing she does is get on her knees before her couch and prays. Then she gets up and called Pastor and Lady Campbell.

"Hello?"

"Hi Pastor, it is Traci Carter."

"Yes, hi, Traci! Is everything all right?"

"Well no, that's why I am calling. Steven got into a fight with Paul and they're both in the hospital. It was bad. Steven ended up having broken ribs and a damaged spleen and a broken nose but I thank God they didn't have to do anything. They say it will heal on its own. I just got home from the hospital a few minutes ago."

"Oh, man. This Paul guy doesn't want to leave you alone."

"No, he doesn't, but it gets worse. He has a concussion of some kind and somehow he woke up thinking I am his wife. The doctor said it's some rare case that's based on your state of mind when you hit your head. He was obsessed and believed I was his."

"What, does Steven know this?"

"No, I'm hoping he'll come back to reality before Steven is well enough to come home. The doctor says that with rest and time we'll see when everything starts to return to him."

"Well, the Mrs. and I will come by the hospital sometime tomorrow and we will be praying for everybody."

"Thank you, Pastor." They hang up. Traci sits there for a few minutes before finally getting up. She hadn't realized how tired she is physically and mentally, and she has to force herself to get up. She's not hungry, so she goes right upstairs, takes a nice shower, and plops into bed. It doesn't take long before she falls asleep.

Traci sleeps through the night, and when she wakes up it's 9:45 in the morning. She jumps up, not realizing what day it is at first. Then everything comes back to her, and she flops back down and lays there.

This is a time when she wishes she had her mom around, but she had kind of drifted away from her and they lost contact. She hated her childhood; her own father didn't want anything to do with her and her mother was always calling him to come over. When he did, she would ask him for money, they would get into an argument, and he would leave. Her mother would end up getting money from one of her other male friends, who she would tell Traci to call "Uncle."

She knew her mother was trying her best. She had a little job, but the pay didn't take care of everything. Traci was determined to go to college to get a better paying job so she wouldn't end up like her mom, depending on men to help her get by. When she did go to college, stripping was the only way she could pay for it.

Traci is about to get up when she thinks about her mother-in-law, so she calls her. "Hello?"

"Hi Mom, it's Traci."

"Hi! You calling to check on Jr.?"

"Yes, and I have to talk to you about Steven."

"What about Steven?" Her voice sounds alarmed.

"I don't know how to say this. Steven is in the hospital...he was in a fight. He ended up with broken ribs and his spleen's a little damaged. I am sorry in my delay in calling you but things were happening so fast."

"A fight, huh? That doesn't sound like my Steven. He's changed from all of that, unless something set him off. What caused him to fight?"

"Well, here is the thing." Traci stops, takes a deep breath, and lets it out. "He was fighting a man that I was seeing."

"What! Are you telling me you're cheating on my son?" Her voice is getting louder.

Traci has to pull the phone away from her ear for a second before answering. "Yes, I was, but Steven and I are now trying to work things out. We even went to counseling with our pastor and his wife."

"What made them fight?" Her tone is slightly condescending.

Traci tries to ignore it and gives her a short version of what happened. "The man became obsessed and started coming by the house. I heard a noise outside so I went to the patio and he was there. He grabbed me to come with him and I hollered out for Steven. Steven punched him in his head for him to let me go. When he did, they started fighting."

"You said he was obsessed with you?"

"Yeah."

"How long were you seeing him?"

"Not that long."

"Is he someone you already knew?"

"Yeah, someone from my past."

"Past? You mean when you were a stripper?"

That hurts Traci, and she has to bite her tongue and remember Steven. "Yes, Helen, actually it is."

"This other man, did Steven hurt him?"

"He's in the hospital too with a concussion, a broken nose and swollen eyes."

"Good."

"I'm going to come by in about a half an hour to get Jr. so you can go to the hospital. Since I don't have anyone else to watch him can you call me when you're home? I'll bring Jr. back and then I'll go to the hospital."

Traci calls her mother-in-law, Helen, to tell her she is on her way to pick up Jr. When she gets there, he is ready. Helen says, "I'll call you when I am home so you can bring Jr back."

Once Helen gets to the hospital, she asks for Steven's room number. When she goes in, she is shocked to see the condition he is in and it's too hard for her to fight back her tears as she watches him sleep.

Steven hears something and opens his swollen, bruised eyes. "Oh, Mom, don't cry. I'll be ok."

"It's hard to see you like this."

"I know." Steven's voice is somewhat weak.

Helen says, "Don't talk too much. Traci told me everything and I can't believe it. You're a hothead and it's hard to calm you down. I am so thankful to God that you didn't need any surgery and you're recovering. She told me she was cheating on you with this person and that y'all were trying to work things out."

"Yeah Mom, we are, and I was just starting to come around. I was staying in the basement but I'm trying to trust her. I'm taking it slow."

"Ok. Steven, you've talked a little too much. I'll come back…get your rest. I love you."

"I love you too, Mom."

Traci gets a call from her mother-in-law telling her that she is home. She also tells her how bad Steven looks and that he sounds weak. "I know," Traci says. "I'll bring Jr. by in an hour. He's just about to eat."

"Ok, but I want to tell you that I mentioned to Steven your infidelity and he said that y'all are trying to work things out. I just wanted to hear that from him."

"I know you haven't approved of him marrying me because of my past, and we haven't gotten along too well. But if Steven is willing to still try to make it work can you and I try too?"

"I just don't want to see my son hurt, but as long as he is willing I am willing to try as well. I'll see you and Jr. soon."

Traci calls Sheila while waiting for Pastor and Lady Campbell to come back from seeing Steven. "Hello?"

"Hey, Sheila. I'm calling to tell you that Steven is in the hospital. He was in another fight with Paul and they're both in the hospital. I'm here now waiting for Pastor and Lady Campbell to come back from seeing Steven."

"Oh my God, when did this happen?"

"This whole thing is a mess. It happened last night."

"Last night! Girl, how come you didn't you call me? Never mind, I'm coming; I'm only five minutes away."

Traci sits there watching TV until Sheila walks in the room. "It feels like I just hung up with you," Traci says.

"I told you I was close by. So what happened to Steven?"

I heard a noise out back so I went to the patio and there Paul was. I told him to leave before Steven saw him and called the cops. But he would not leave; he believed I hadn't been calling him because of Steven. I told him no, we are working on our marriage. He did not like that so he grabbed me and tried to drag me away. I hollered out for Steven, and when he came out he saw Paul with his arms around my neck. He told him to let me go but he refused, so Steven walked up to him and punched him in his head a few times trying to make him defend himself and let me go. Girl, they got out of control. They wouldn't listen to me so I called the cops, and a few of my neighbors heard me hollering and the crashing of the furniture so they came out to try to stop them. Steven has broken ribs and a damaged spleen from Paul kicking him, a broken nose, and swollen eyes. Paul also has a broken nose, swollen eyes, and he has a concussion. He came to the hospital unconscious. But this is the kicker—when he came to he was asking for his wife."

"He's married?"

"No, girl…he was calling *me* his wife!"

"No! What! Oh no, this is crazy."

Traci asks what's going on with her. "John came over the other day to tell me he decided he wants to try to make things work with Jasmine because of the baby. He said he doesn't want his son growing up without him. Do you believe this? I gave that man ten years of my life. I wanted to have his child. Oh, Traci that hurts. I really can't stand her right now and to think I have to work with her. She stole everything from me."

Just then the waiting room door opens, and they both look up as Jasmine walks in. Sheila jumps up. "What are *you* doing here, you homewrecker? It's bad enough that I have to work with you! What, you here to gloat that you have my husband?" Sheila is so loud that she can be heard in the hallway. Traci is in such shock from Sheila's behavior that she can't react fast enough. She gets up, puzzled that Sheila knows Jasmine.

Pastor and Lady Campbell are making their way back to the waiting room when they hear the commotion. As they walk in, they hear Traci saying to Sheila, "Calm down. How do you know her?"

With tears in her eyes that she refuses to let fall, Sheila says just as loudly, "She's the one John chose over me because of the baby!" She's the one that's ruining my life."

Neither Traci nor Sheila sees Pastor and Lady Campbell come into the room until they hear Pastor's voice. Jasmine is about to pop off, hand raised and her finger pointed. "First of all—"

"I know these are not my church members making a commotion in this hospital," comes a man's authoritative voice, sounding almost like Bishop T. D. Jakes, out of nowhere. Traci and Sheila stop and turn around.

"What is going on here?" Pastor says in a chastising manner.

"Oh Pastor, I'm sorry for my behavior. But she's the one John's been seeing and he just told me that he wants to be with her for the baby's sake. Plus, she's the receptionist in my office. I've just had enough."

"Ok, Sheila." Lady Campbell leads her to a seat and rubs her back. "It is going to be ok."

While Traci introduces Jasmine to Pastor, she says, "She's also the ex of the man I was seeing. They have a five-year-old daughter together. I had to contact someone to represent him. I found their picture in his wallet and her number in his phone, so I called her."

Pastor says, "Let's have a seat." He leads Jasmine to the other end of the room and asks if she's ok.

"I think so…it is just all the excitement." She rubs her stomach.

"Is it ok if I talk to you?"

"Yeah, it's ok."

"Do you have someone you can talk to like a pastor? Do you belong to a church?"

"No," Jasmine says, tears in her eyes. She doesn't know if it's her hormones or something else. "Sheila used to talk to me. She even told me I should talk to you and your wife. She gave me your number. But, well…that was before all this. I really didn't know that John was her husband."

"If I may say so, it doesn't matter who his wife is. He's still married and that should have made him hands off."

"Yes, that's true, but I didn't know he was married at first. And when he finally told me that he was, my feelings were already way too involved."

"I understand completely, but it still doesn't make it right."

"Yeah, but if he knows he is married he should have told me."

"If I may say this to you, and please excuse me if I offend you, but let me explain something to you. No man is going to tell a woman his status, especially if he feels he might get some. My wife can talk to you from a woman's side, and I can tell it to you straight. I would really love to talk to you more." He reaches in his breast pocket, pulls out a card, and hands it to her. "This is my card. It has the office number at my church and my home number."

Jasmine takes it. "Thank you. I really will call you."

"Please do. I believe we can truly help you." A single tear slides down Jasmine's face, and she wipes it away quickly.

Pastor calls for his wife to come over. "Do you mind if she gives you a hug?" Jasmine's answer is slow and a little unsure but she finally says no. When Lady Campbell hugs her tightly, her tears began to flow and she feels a little awkward. She doesn't know why she's crying.

Lady Campbell lets her go after a while. "Everything will be all right. Just trust and believe in God."

Pastor Campbell says, "I gave her a card and she said she will come by to talk to us."

Lady Campbell says, "That's good. I'll look forward to talking with her." She says to Jasmine, "Well, you have a good day, and remember: put your trust in God." She and Pastor walk over to Traci and Sheila, and five minutes later they leave.

"Hello?"

"Hey Traci, it's Sheila."

"I'm calling to see how Steven is doing and to apologize for my behavior on the other day."

"The doctor says Steven is recovering well. He's still in pain, but that is to be expected."

"Do they know when he can come home?"

"No, not yet."

"I've been asking you about Steven and I never

asked you how you are holding up."

"Thanks. I think I am just going through the motions with the back and forth to the hospital and with Steven Jr. and his mother."

"What about his mother?"

"Girl, she never liked me because of my past. She always acted as if I wasn't good enough for him. When I called her to tell her what happened, she wanted to know who and why he was fighting."

"Stop playing. What did you tell her?"

"The truth. I said he was fighting someone from my past. She had the nerve to say, 'You mean when you were a stripper?'"

"Uh-uh, she said that?"

"Girl, it took everything in me to refrain myself from giving her a tongue-lashing. I had to think of Steven to stop myself. Plus, I needed her to watch Steven Jr. Tell you the truth, I wish I could tell my mom all this."

"I know, but at least yours is still living," And you can go to her house to see if she's still living there and try to reconnect with her. Sheila says. "My mom is gone and I still deeply miss her. "Traci, look, you're grown and you've overcome many things to become the woman that you are. You're not a little girl; you're a strong beautiful woman now. It's time to heal old wounds from your past."

"Yeah. Ah, I guess you're right."

Traci changes the subject back and says, "Steven's mother had the nerve to say she asked Steven about this."

"No!"

"She told me she wanted to hear it from him."

"What?"

"Oh, that we are trying to work things out."

"Girl, she is a piece of work."

"Tell me about it."

"But in the end I asked her that, if he is willing to work things out with me, could she and I do the same. She said that if he is willing then she is too."

"Oh, well, that's good."

"Yeah but I will be glad when Steven comes home."

"Did you take Little Steven to see his dad?"

"Oh, yeah, and maybe I should not have done that."

"Why, what happened?"

"Little Steven cried something terrible and I had to have him sleep with me last night. I need to tell Jazz…oh, I'm sorry, Sheila."

"No, it is ok. What are you going to tell her?"

"Do not bring her daughter to the hospital. I know her situation is different…he doesn't know her so it might be worse. By the way, I saw her earlier and she told me she's sorry for everything and that she agreed to meet with Pastor. She said she needs some help and that you and her used to talk and you told her about Pastor."

"Yeah, we both shared some things with each other and she said she could use some advice. I told her about Pastor and gave her the church phone number."

ABOUT THE AUTHOR

Carmen Yvette Jones is a Christian and self-published author. Born and raised in Southwest Philadelphia, Pennsylvania, and the youngest of five, she is the mother of two sons, Joseph and Frank. Carmen is reserved and easygoing, she has a heart for women and has found a way to be heard and connect with other women through writing.

OTHER BOOKS BY CARMEN YVETTE JONES

THE TRUTH ABOUT US:
Words to Inspire & Encourage
issued September 2016

Purchase online:
www.amazon.com
www.bn.com
www.booksamillion.com

CARMEN YVETTE JONES

Made in the USA
Middletown, DE
08 March 2023